THE LAST COLLAR

ALSO BY LAWRENCE KELTER & FRANK ZAFIRO
The Last Collar
No Dibs on Murder

ALSO BY LAWRENCE KELTER

My Cousin Vinny Series
My Cousin Vinny   *Wing and a Prayer*
Back to Brooklyn

Stephanie Chalice Thrillers
(includes the Prequel Series, Main Series, and City Beat Thrillers)
Chloe Mather Thrillers

Other Novels
Counterblow   *Season of Faith*
Kiss of the Devil's Breath   *Out of Ashes*
Palindrome   *Lexa's War*
Encrypting Maya   *The Treasure*
Saving Cervantes   *The Whale*

As Editor
The Black Car Business Volume 1   *Writers Crushing COVID-19*
The Black Car Business Volume 2

ALSO BY FRANK ZAFIRO
River City series
Stefan Kopriva Mysteries
SpoCompton series
Charlie-316 series (with Colin Conway)
Bricks & Cam Jobs (with Eric Beetner)
The Ania Series (with Jim Wilsky)

Other Novels
The Last Horseman   *An Unlikely Phoenix*
Some Degree of Murder (with *Chisolm's Debt*
Colin Conway)   *The Trade Off (w/ B.R. Paulson)*
At This Point in My LIfe   *The Ride-Along (forthcoming)*

LAWRENCE KELTER & FRANK ZAFIRO

THE LAST COLLAR

Copyright © 2017 by Lawrence Kelter & Frank Scalise
Second edition: 2021 by Code 4 Press, an imprint of Frank Zafiro, LLC
First edition: 2017 by Down and Out Books

All rights reserved. No part of the book may be reproduced in any form or by any electronic or mechanical means, including information storage and retrieval systems, without permission in writing from the publisher, except by a reviewer who may quote brief passages in a review.

The characters and events in this book are fictitious. Any similarity to real persons, living or dead, is coincidental and not intended by the author.

ISBN: 9798733645582

For all the cops who get it right.

Chapter One

Discarded lottery tickets: Mega Millions, Powerball, and scratch-offs of every variety littered the desk behind which the body of Jessica Lynn Shannon was found. They may not have been winners but the lottery tickets got a second chance at usefulness as bookmarks and notepaper. It didn't stop there—she had fashioned the cardboard scratch-offs into airplanes and the Powerball receipts into miniature macramé animals, giraffes and swans mostly. Her other creations lacked a long elegant neck but they too were masterpieces in their own right.

Me, I was born with ten thumbs and could never fashion anything as intricate as the victim's macramé creations. My dexterity began and ended with popping the top off a cold one.

My partner Matt Winslow was a regular kind of guy, affable and easy-going, with a swelling belly he was constantly trying to hide from our CO. Not quite a run of the mill detective, but then with twenty-four years under his belt...well, who could blame a cop who had the finish line in sight? If it were me, I'd be wolfing down bagels and getting afternoon massages. Sometimes I envied the simplicity of his life: a doting wife, a rugged jock son, and a daughter who always had her nose in a book.

He glanced up at me. "Someone was hoping to get lucky," he astutely diagnosed.

"Yeah, I don't know, these things are a gigantic waste of time. I just hand the cashier a twenty and then chuck the ticket in the garbage before leaving the store."

Winslow wrinkled his nose. "You're kidding, John? You don't bother checking 'em?"

"Nah. Who needs all that money anyway? It only causes problems. Half of it gets taxed right off the bat. Then long lost relatives crawl out of the woodwork and you find friends you didn't know existed. Forget about the charities, they'll slither so far up your ass you'll need a coat hanger to yank 'em out. Look at all the trouble it brought this poor woman." I could see from the expression on his face that Winslow was secretly hoping I had saved all the lottery tickets and was going to bequeath them to him, an untapped fortune just lying in an old cigar box. "Of course I check them. You think I'm some kind of schmuck?"

"Bastard," Winslow muttered, only half serious.

We turned back to the victim. Jessica Shannon was much too young to die. I'd already fished through her pocketbook and knew that she was just thirty-two years old, a little bit of a thing wrapped in Nike spandex, wearing well-worn running shoes, with a figure capable of bringing the most devoutly faithful husband to his knees.

"The poor thing," Winslow lamented. "Pretty face."

I was wondering how he could tell. Bruises mottled the victim's throat, faint dabs of purple and yellow where finger pressure had bruised the tender flesh on her elegantly slender neck and rendered revealing ligature marks. Her eyes bulged from their sockets, a telltale sign of asphyxia, and her face was frozen, a sardonic sculpture that told a story even a fledgling investigator could recognize. Her tongue was extended and hung from the side of her open mouth. Still, I understood what Winslow was getting at. Her fixed stare eyes were still the most intense shade of emerald green I'd ever seen. She must've been absolutely stunning before asphyxia caused the corneas of her eyes to swell with ugly red blood vessels. Her skin was porcelain white and her hair...yes, of course, it was an intensely deep shade of red like an animal whose pelt fetched thousands. "This Irish sod must've been one fair lass."

"And she had some hot bod, huh?"

"*Really?* A woman is dead of asphyxia, her face looks as distressed as Han Solo's when he was sealed in carbonite, and that's the next thing to pop into your head?" I sighed a manly sigh. "But you're right. Calories probably slid through her GI tract like they were coated with Teflon."

"You've got some way with words. They ought to name you the unofficial poet of Brooklyn South, Mocha." Winslow was tall; he knelt to get a better look at the victim—actually, with his growing midsection he was still an arm's length away. "Think she already went for her run?"

"I don't know. Why don't you give her armpits a quick sniff so we know for sure?"

"Very funny, dickhead." He raised his finger and pointed at a spot just below the bra line. "See that. She already finished."

Winslow was perceptive. There was a white stain on the hot pink Lycra fabric where her sweat had dried and left the slightest residue of salt. "Maybe she fell behind on the laundry."

"Women don't do that," he scoffed. "Only guys wear their shit more than once. A woman wears something for ten minutes, changes her mind about the outfit, and chucks it straight into the hamper. I've got two of them of them at home and believe me I know."

"Well look at you getting all *Vogue* on me. Who knew you were such an expert on women's hygiene. What do you use for vaginal itch?"

He grabbed his crotch. "I got the cure right here."

"More like the cause, ain't it?"

He flipped me the bird, which was well deserved and long overdue. "Enough. Mocha, a woman is dead here."

"Hey, you started it."

"Well, time to get serious now."

"You're my conscience, Winslow. I've always relied on your quiet inner strength to keep me on the straight and narrow."

"The hell does that mean?"

We'd been partners way too long and had seen more than our fair share of cooling corpses. Humor was our defense mechanism. It kept us from going bat shit crazy when we were knee-deep in cadavers. "Okay, let's get down and dirty. She's fully dressed so sex doesn't appear to be the motive."

"We can't rule out oral."

"No, Matt, we can't but I don't see a woman getting strangled over a crappy BJ—if such a thing even exists."

"Yeah. Probably not." Winslow stood and backed away while keeping his eyes trained on the victim. "Can I make an observation?"

"Her position?"

"Exactly. She's sitting back in the chair—it's almost as if she was positioned that way. Common sense would tell us that she should be slumped over but she's not. Instead, she's sitting right up against her desk, almost as if her chair had been pushed in for her."

I swept my gaze over the scene. He was right.

"And you know it's damn near impossible to strangle someone from behind. Not unless the doer has incredibly strong hands."

He was right again. It's not easy to keep adequate pressure on the arteries long enough to cut off blood flow to the brain with the thumbs behind the head. The other fingers tire too quickly. It's the thumb that has all the strength. "He could've used his forearms. Like the choke hold they taught us at the academy."

Winslow shook his head. "Look at those ligature marks. Those are definitely finger marks."

Right a third time. Winslow was on a roll.

"So with the posed position here, you figure she was murdered elsewhere and placed at her desk for a reason?"

"Yup."

"Like a tableau?"

"Yeah, Matt, like that."

The house faced Marine Park in a high-rent section of Brooklyn. "A girl with physical attributes like hers, I'm sure any number of red-blooded men noticed her running through the park. Let's get a detail out on the street right away...and check with her neighbors, too."

Her sister had stopped by to pick her up for lunch and had discovered the body. She let herself in and walked around the house when the doorbell wasn't answered—she found her sister motionless in the chair.

All the lottery tickets made me think. "What's a place like this worth, Matt?"

"Buck and a half. I don't know, maybe higher." He shrugged, considering further. "In this area...maybe two million."

"So what's with all the lottery tickets? You think maybe a rich woman was down on her luck?"

"Very possible that she fell on hard times. The economy isn't exactly chugging along these days."

"Or maybe she owed someone a lot of money."

Winslow made a doubtful face. "Someone who got tired of waiting for repayment?"

"Yeah, I know. Maybe not. But I think the money angle is still a good one. Look at that old clunky computer monitor on her desk—I don't see someone with disposable income working in front of a relic like that, you?"

Winslow shook his head. "I wonder if she was working on something." He walked around behind her and clicked the mouse with a glove-clad hand. His eyes grew wide.

"What's there?"

He motioned for me to join him. A solitary word was typed on an otherwise blank page. In bold type, red letters, and caps it read: BITCH!

Chapter Two

Bernie Collier stared at the screen for a few more seconds, then pushed up his glasses, and turned to us. "It's a word processor document."

"I know."

"Microsoft Word, to be precise. Pretty ubiquitous."

I suppressed a frown. Bernie and his hundred-dollar vocabulary. "Look, I know that's what it is. I just—"

"Yeah, asshole," Winslow interjected. "We know about computers. We aren't idiots, or—"

"Troglodytes?"

Another C-note word for the Bernster.

"We're looking for anything you can recover," I said. "For starters, forensics can dust the keyboard and maybe we'll get lucky on prints there."

Bernie gave me a doubtful look.

I shrugged. "We gotta try. But we need a forensic review of her system, both on her local drive and any online activity."

"I assumed that's why I was summoned on my day off," Bernie said.

"Your day..." Winslow's mouth fell open, and he looked over at me. "You believe this guy?"

Bernie ignored him, and reached into his large equipment bag. I was no computer whiz, but I knew enough to get the gist of what he was going to do. He'd get an imprint of the entire system on another external drive, one that was forensically sound and met the evidence standard for court. Then he'd save all open files, power down the system and seize the desktop. The equipment back at the lab would do a better job of exploring everything on the hard drive, even deleted files. Same was true for investigating Jessica Shannon's online footprint.

I pulled Winslow a few feet away to let Bernie work and keep my partner from smacking him.

"Son of a bitch," Winslow muttered.

"I know."

"The girl's dead, Mocha. Murdered. And he acts like he's missing something more important. Probably a goddamn Dungeons and Dragons tournament."

"Yeah."

"Asshole."

"Without a doubt."

Winslow turned his gaze to me. "Don't do that."

"Don't do what?"

"You're patronizing me."

"No, I'm not."

"You are. You definitely are. Stop it."

"All right."

"I mean it, man. I have a wife to do that for me. I don't need you pitching in."

I shrugged. Sarah didn't patronize him, as far as I could tell. Nagged him a little about his weight, but only from a health perspective. She loved him and, okay, I guess she was a bit of a nudge but if I had a grain of rice for every time she told him how good looking he was, I could feed the world.

That made me smile. Maybe she actually *did* patronize him a little.

"Now *you're* smiling. What?"

"Nothing, you ugly prick. Let's get back on point here."

"I was never off. You were."

"Fine," I said, in the most patronizing voice I could muster.

I could tell Winslow really wanted to flip me off again, but with all of the forensic unit techs working the scene and the patrol rookie standing

The Last Collar

at the door with a log sheet, he resisted. "Well, *Detective*, let's backtrack."

"My thoughts exactly. Go ahead."

"Even without the computer message, you know this thing had to be personal, right?"

"Sure. Strangulation is almost always personal."

"So I'm thinking someone close to her somehow."

"Odds are, yeah. But that doesn't necessarily mean *she* knew they were close."

"Stalker?"

"Can't rule it out."

Winslow half-shrugged. "Maybe. But I don't think so."

I didn't either. I only brought it up so we could look at it, bat it around, and probably set it aside. Every investigation is a dance, and you can't leave out the steps. "Because no forced entry?"

"Yeah. And no sex. Those stalker types, it's almost always sexual for them. Even if they can't get it up or follow through, at least the pose is sexual. But here?" He gestured toward Jessica Shannon's body. "Still dressed, and posed in a way that's...how would you call it? Simple?"

"Mundane," Bernie interjected.

Winslow scowled. "No one asked you,

Scrabble-head."

Bernie seemed to ignore him, instead tapping a few keys. His shoulder was only a foot away from the victim's. Then he said, "Words are important, Detective. They have power." He glanced up, first at Jessica, then at Winslow. "And not just for clerics in D&D."

Winslow opened his mouth to reply but I pulled him further away. "This is getting us nowhere," I told him.

"Little IT weasel," Winslow muttered.

"Leave it alone."

"He gets under my skin. I hate it when someone can do that."

I thought about what Bernie said. If the word on the computer screen had been something unique, I'd have agreed with him on the importance. But "bitch" wasn't very imaginative. It was...well, it was mundane.

"If it wasn't a stranger stalking her, a boyfriend is the best bet."

"The sister would know about that."

"Hope so."

"So how do you want to go at this?" Winslow asked.

"Your call."

He shook his head. "Nope. You're lead."

The Last Collar

"No, I'm not. You're up next on the wheel. It's your turn."

"Uh-uh. I had the last one. The Ferguson widow."

"That was a ground ball."

"It was more like a slow roller to the mound. But every one counts. So you're lead, and it's your call. What do you want to do?"

The beginnings of a headache pulsed behind my left eye. I clenched my jaw and rubbed my temple while I thought about Winslow's question. "We'll talk to the sister, and see what the canvass gets us. If nothing there, we can check into the rest of the family and close associates while we wait for the forensics to come back. Get a subpoena for financial records, too."

"The executor can give us permission for those. We don't need a subpoena."

Winslow hated paperwork.

"Maybe so, but a subpoena or even a search warrant is ironclad in court."

"Fine," he conceded. "You type it up, though."

I always did, but I resisted saying so. "We do all that, and somewhere in there, we ought to catch a loose thread."

Winslow sighed. "Why do I even ask? Same approach, every time with you."

"Something works for me, I stick with it."

Winslow didn't argue. He couldn't. I was a case-solving motherfucker, the be-all-and-end-all of homicide investigation, with a reputation known so far and wide that perps would line up at the station house steps just to turn themselves in. Okay, now I'm just talking shit but you've gotta love a cop with bit of swagger in his step.

The point is that I'm good, damn good, and Winslow knew it.

"Let's get coffee while they finish up processing the scene," I said. "Then we can talk to the sister and do another walk-through."

"I thought you wanted to canvass."

"Let the uniforms do it. If they get anybody worth talking to, we'll interview them."

"Sounds good to me. There's a diner six blocks over. We'll drive over. It's kinda old-school, though. They might not have your prissy little special coffee."

"You talking about the Greek place? Niko's?"

"That's the one."

I gave him a grin. "They've entered the twenty-first century, Matt. They know about mochas."

He sighed. "The whole world is falling part. Why can't you just drink it like a regular cop—strong and black?"

"Like *you're* regular? Why do we have this conversation every time coffee comes up?"

"Because it ain't right," Winslow said, but he gave up. "You want to drive?"

I didn't, but before I could reply, a gravelly voice broke in behind us. "You two limp dicks aren't going anywhere."

Chapter Three

I'd recognize Coltrane's bulldog rumble with my head submersed in a toilet. He had a voice so deep it could pulverize kidney stones. He was a dark-skinned Adonis, six-four with a polished noggin and muscles on top of muscles. Add a cape and mask and the man was a goddamn superhero.

Or more to the point, a super villain.

Lieutenant Coltrane worked out four times a week at a real-man's gym, and ate the same healthy, boring crap every day: steamed chicken, brown rice, and broccoli from The Golden Dragon, the chop suey joint down the block from the precinct house.

The lieutenant and I got along about as well as any detective and his commanding officer, which is to say not great. But for some reason he really got to Winslow. Maybe it was Coltrane's massive size. I'm not sure what triggered this reaction but whenever the lieutenant came around, my partner got this look on his face akin to if a surgeon was about to snip his vas deferens.

"What's with the coffee break shit?" Coltrane snapped. "There's plenty of water in the bathroom sink." I wish he was just messing with us, and maybe somewhere in the bowels of his microscopic personality, he was. The man was a natural born ball-breaker, an ex-marine who had made his bones beating down street thugs in Bed-Stuy back in the days when you could still get away with that shit. Once he became boss, he was certain that we all still behaved that way but had simply become more adept at covering it up.

"We're at a natural break point," I said. "Gotta let forensics do their thing."

"Break point, huh?" He eyed me suspiciously. "Good. You've got time to run it for me, then."

"We're still waiting on Sergeant Gastineau," I said, looking around in vain for him. Just like the Ghost not to show up when we could use him to run interference.

Coltrane ignored my comment, sniffing the air. "Smells like shit in here."

"The deceased evacuated her bowels," I said. "It's fairly common in homicides."

It was a slight dig, and Coltrane knew it. He promoted quickly, doing only a short stint as a detective before making sergeant, and then lieutenant, both in rapid succession. He spent his time as a detective in Vice, so he knew more about hookers and blowjob queens in drag than he did about dead bodies.

And I liked reminding him of that.

He glared at me for a moment, and I thought he might tear into me right there, but instead, he turned to the deceased and snapped on some blue gloves. "Give us the room," he said loudly. The forensics geeks knew he was talking to them and took five, leaving him alone in the room with Winslow and me. Only Collier remained behind, still tapping at his keyboard.

"That's better," Coltrane said. "Couldn't hear myself think." He turned to us. "What've you two geniuses figured out?"

"The victim's name is Jessica Shannon," Winslow swallowed hard and began to speak. "It was an inside job."

"How do you know?"

"She lived alone. No signs of forced entry. Doesn't appear that robbery was the motive nor does it appear to be a sex crime. The victim may have had financial difficulties."

"Where'd you get that?"

He pointed at all the discarded lottery tickets.

The Last Collar

"Rich people can't play the lottery?" Coltrane asked.

"Sure," Winslow said. "If they want. It's just, well..."

"In our experience, they don't," I interjected.

Coltrane's gaze flicked to me. "No, huh?"

I shook my head. "Rich people are better at math, I guess."

Coltrane smirked but motioned for Winslow to continue.

Winslow cleared his throat. "Uh, cause of death appears to be asphyxiation—there are ligature marks on her throat consistent with manual strangulation. The body seems posed. We think she might've been murdered elsewhere and moved to her desk post-mortem."

Coltrane spoke without diverting his gaze from the victim. "And that, to you, seems like a complete investigation?"

"No," I said. "It was just time for coffee."

Coltrane shook his head in mild disgust and continued to examine the crime scene. "There's a perspiration stain on her top. Either of you two masterminds speak to joggers in the park?"

"On our to-do list, Lieutenant," I said, flinching inwardly. Like either of us needed investigative tips from Coltrane.

"After your coffee break, right?"

"We're already assigning men to the park and preparing copies of the victim's photo."

"So I guess we move onto interviews," he said as he peeled off his gloves.

No kidding, Sherlock, I thought, but didn't say. *You only want to push back against Coltrane so hard.*

He rolled on. "That means neighbors, relatives, co-workers, and friends. Explore the financial angle, too. Call what's his name in forensic accounting and get him on this."

"Davis?" Winslow offered.

"Yeah. Davis. He's sharper than the other guy..."

"Braverman?" Winslow queried.

"Yeah, Braverman. That mope can barely tell a balance sheet from a grocery list." Coltrane finally turned and faced us. "Let's see what turns up in terms of DNA. And you," he said as he glanced at Collier. "We'll need a breakdown on the computer hard drive, stat."

Collier winked and gave him a thumbs-up. "Indubitably."

I gave Collier a sour look. "What's a hundred-dollar word for brown-nose?"

"Sycophant," Collier answered immediately.

Winslow shrugged. "Bootlick?"

"I like bootlick better. Well done, my partner."

"Enough!" Coltrane snapped. He pointed at Winslow and me, scowling. "Get serious and get to work. I want some results here. This isn't some doper who OD'd in a goddamn alley."

Neither of us answered, and after a moment, he turned on his heel and stalked out of the room. Winslow and I stood there, listening to his descending footfalls, followed by the front door slamming closed.

"That guy," Winslow muttered, "is a raging asshole."

I shrugged. "Coltrane is what he is. Spending too much energy on it is a waste."

"Thanks, Confucius."

"Welcome."

Sergeant Pete Gastineau wandered through the door from another room. I gaped at him, unaware he'd arrived on scene. He held two cups of coffee in his hands, and a fragile, eager look on his face like a dog who just knew he was going to be kicked. "How's it going, guys?"

"Wow," I said. "Your timing is just amazing."

The Ghost always seemed to be out of the line of fire, letting us take the full brunt of Coltrane. Being a sergeant, it was his job to run our squad, and to keep the lieutenant both informed and at bay. Instead, all he was good at was being invisible.

He extended both cups toward us. "This one's a mocha," he said to me, giving the left hand cup a raise.

I glanced at Winslow. "Come on," I said. "We've got an interview to do." We brushed past the Ghost, leaving him holding both cups and staring after us, bewildered.

Chapter Four

Standing by the window, Morgan Shannon struck me as a pale imitation of her sister. Her skin was an almost unhealthy white, her curves weren't as round, and her eyes seemed slightly dull. Even her hair lacked the lustrous sheen of her sister's, and instead resembled roughly spun copper.

Jesus, I thought. *I really am getting cold. She just stumbled upon her dead sister. Of course she looks like hell. How would I look if I dropped in on my folks and found them murdered?*

But I knew the answer. The cop in me would always win out. I'd stay focused, take it in stride. It was who I was, for better or worse.

Mostly worse.

Less than two hours had passed since we had arrived at the crime scene. Morgan had waited patiently until we were ready for her. Winslow took lead on the interview. We always played it by ear on who did the questioning, depending on what the witness, victim, or suspect needed at the time. Sometimes it was an older brother. Old married guy that he was, Winslow pumped out that vibe like an oil spill. He could also turn on the bad, suspicious cop routine pretty effectively. My specialty was to be the knight in shining armor. Or the flirt. Or the good cop, the one who wanted to believe you.

"My sister?" Morgan Shannon asked as we approached her in the living room.

As ridiculous as it sounded, I knew she was asking if Jessica were somehow still alive. She was holding onto that last vestige of hope that she had been wrong, and the professionals had miraculously come in and cleared up the matter.

Winslow gave a small shake of his head, and took her hand. "I'm sorry for your loss."

Morgan held on for a long second, silent, her lip quivering. Tears streamed from her eyes. Then she let loose a wail and collapsed into Winslow's arms. He held her, patting her shoulder and making soothing noises.

I had to give it up for the guy. He could be an asshole at times, but he was great with victims. He wouldn't want me or anyone else to know it, but he really cared. I did, too, in my own way, but I think his caring went much deeper.

We waited for a few minutes while Morgan

sobbed on Winslow's chest. After a time, her sobs declined, until there was just an occasional hitch. He waited a minute or two longer, then put his hands on her upper arms and moved her back. I'd scavenged some tissues while she was crying and held them out to her. She gave me a small, grateful smile through her sad eyes and took them.

"We have to ask you a couple of questions, Miss Shannon," Winslow said.

She nodded as she wiped her eyes and nose. "Of course. I understand. Anything I can do to help."

They sat down.

"Can I smoke?" Morgan asked.

"Of course."

While she fumbled in her purse for her cigarettes, I took up a position off to the side where I could observe her while Winslow asked the questions. When our roles were reversed, he always took out his notebook and made notes, but I didn't want to cause a distraction. Besides, I had a good memory.

Morgan found her cigarettes, lit one, and took a deep drag. She let the smoke out in a billowing rush.

Winslow dove into the interview. "Are you Jessica's only sibling?"

She nodded, swallowing with difficulty.

"Are you the younger sister?"

"No, the older. By two years. But everyone thought she was older."

"Why's that?"

Morgan shrugged. "She just acted that way, I guess. More responsible. More...steady."

"Did she have a boyfriend?"

"Until recently. They broke up a few weeks ago."

Winslow's gaze flicked imperceptibly to me for a brief second. I knew what he was thinking. An angry ex-boyfriend was a potential jackpot in a case like this.

"What's his name?" he asked.

"Arturo. He's an artist."

"And how long did they date?"

She took a deep breath, thinking. "Oh, I don't know exactly. Six months maybe? Could have been a little longer."

"Was it serious?"

"I don't think so. I think..." she hesitated.

Winslow reached out and patted her hand. "It's all right, Morgan. Anything you can tell us is helpful."

She let out a shuddering breath and dabbed her eyes with the tissue. "I just don't want to say anything bad about her. I loved my sister, and now she's...*gone*," she blubbered.

"What is it you don't want to say?"

She put the cigarette to her lips with a shaking hand. "It's not even bad. Hell, she did all the right things, followed all the rules, even the stupid ones. She deserved to have some fun."

"That's what Arturo was? A fling?"

Her gaze rose to meet Winslow's and her eyes flashed angrily. "See? You make it sound like something tawdry. That's what I was trying to avoid."

Winslow shook his head. "Someone finding some happiness in this world isn't tawdry. At least, I don't think it is."

"No?"

"Not at all."

Morgan nodded in slow agreement. "You're right, of course. Though I don't think our parents would agree on that point."

Winslow nodded that he understood. "Just so I'm clear, the thing with Arturo was what you might call casual?"

"That's my impression."

"And you're close enough with your sister that you'd know?"

A slight flash of anger passed through her expression again. Her lips pressed together momentarily and I was struck with the idea that I would probably see that same expression again when we met her mother.

"Of course. We were sisters."

Winslow held up his hands apologetically. "Sorry. I have to ask. Not every family is close, you know?"

Her expression softened slightly. "Well, we were."

"That's good." He scratched his chin in thought, though I knew it was an affectation. Then he asked, "Did Arturo believe it was casual, do you think?"

She thought about that for a few seconds, then shrugged. "I'm not sure. Jessie didn't talk about that part of their relationship much."

"If you had to guess."

"If I had to guess, I'd say he probably enjoyed the benefits of having a wealthy girlfriend with no strings attached."

"Do you know Arturo's last name?"

"Calderas."

"And an address?"

She shook her head. "Sorry. Every time I ever met him was either here or out somewhere."

Winslow nodded. "Okay. Let's move on. Did Jessie—"

Morgan held up her hand. "Please don't call her that."

Winslow looked confused. "Okay..."

"I know I did just now, but she hated it. I was the only one who called her that. I'd...I'd like to keep it that way."

"Fair enough. Did Jessica work?"

"No. At least, not in the sense that *you* mean it. She wasn't employed, but she did a lot of charity work."

"For which charities?"

"Oh, God. A half-dozen different ones. They'd be in her address book, or you should find some checks she's written them. She supported her charities with both time and money."

"Anything strange happen with any of those charities recently?"

"Not that I know of."

"Anyone angry with Jessica? Maybe she ended her support, or something like that?"

"I don't believe so."

"How was her relationship with your parents?"

Morgan's expression hardened. "Better than mine. Jessie was always the good girl, and our parents treated her accordingly. I was the wild child by comparison. Jessie played by the rules. My parents doted on her."

"Was this an issue between you and them? Or with you and your sister?"

Morgan shook her head. "No, but that's because there wasn't that big of a difference in their affections. They still loved me. They just loved Jessica more."

Winslow hesitated, not seeming to know what to make of that.

"Don't look surprised, Detective," Morgan said. "All parents have a favorite child. Anyone who denies it is lying."

Winslow still didn't answer. I wondered if he was thinking about his son and daughter and trying to deter-mine if she was right.

"It's not like it mattered much. I don't care if my parents approve of me. And, to be fair, the whole dynamic was diffused because of how Jessie handled it."

"How was that?" Winslow managed.

"She idolized me. Treated me like I was a rock star. That seemed to counter-balance my parents' disapproval."

Winslow nodded. "All right. Anything else I should know about your parents and Jessica?"

"No, I think that sums it up."

"Okay." Winslow paused for a beat, and I knew what was coming. He'd gotten the background information first so that if Morgan broke down during the next part of the interview, he still had the information. It was a smart tactic, and one we'd often used.

Morgan seemed to sense something was about to happen. She crushed out her cigarette and gave Winslow her full attention.

"I need you to take me through what happened today," Winslow said. "Step by step."

"Okay," she said, her voice betraying some trepidation.

"When did you arrive this morning?"

"About ten-thirty."

"And was there any particular reason you stopped by?"

"Yes. We were going to get an early lunch and then either go shopping or see a movie."

"Which movie?"

"Excuse me?"

"Which movie were you going to see?"

"Oh." She thought about it for a second. "The romantic comedy with the guy from that hospital show on TV? I don't know the name. Jessie wanted to see it."

"All right. When you got here, was the door locked?"

"I think so. It was closed, and I used my key to

open it. I guess it could have been unlocked, but I don't think so."

"Was anything out of place when you came inside?"

"Not that I could see."

"What did you do next?"

"I called for Jessie. She...she didn't answer me." Tears welled up in her eyes again. She wiped them away with the tissue, then reached for her purse. "I'm sorry," she whispered.

"It's all right," Winslow said.

Morgan dug in her purse and pulled out her cigarettes again. With shaking hands, she lit one, then faced Winslow again. "What else do you want to know?"

"What happened after you called out for Jessica?"

"When she didn't answer, I thought she might be in the shower, or still asleep."

"Did she often sleep late?"

"Almost never. She'd get up early, have coffee and a light breakfast, then go for a run."

"What's early mean?"

"Six or seven, I'd guess. I'm not sure. I'm the late sleeper, so all I know is whenever one of us sleeps over, she's up long before I am."

"Where does she run?"

"Through the park."

"Did the two of you ever run together?"

Morgan shook her head. "No. I don't like to run, so I usually use the rowing machine for my cardio. That, and rock climbing. I tried to get her to try it, too, but Jessie was too dainty for that. Even the practice wall at the gym was too much for her."

"Okay," Winslow said. "What happened once you called out for her and she didn't answer?"

"I wandered around the house, checking the bedroom and the bathroom."

"Did you wonder if she might have gone out?"

"Of course. But her coat was on the rack, and her keys were in the dish by the door. That struck me as odd. So I checked all of the rooms, and that's when I found her."

Tears spilled over her lids and streaked her cheeks. The cigarette between her fingers quivered.

"Did you touch anything?" Winslow asked.

Her face contorted as she fought back a sob. "I grabbed her by the shoulders and shook her." She looked up at Winslow. "Like I could wake her up or something? But I could see...I could see..." She broke off, swallowing another sob.

Winslow patted her on the knee. "All right, Morgan. That's all. We're finished."

"I'm sorry," she said, trying very hard not to sob.

"No, *I'm* sorry," Winslow said. "I'm sorry to have to ask you these questions."

She shook her head. "Don't be," she said, her voice thick. "You do whatever you have to do to catch the son of a bitch who did this."

"I will," Winslow whispered. Then he glanced over at me. "We will."

Chapter Five

I guess the interview with Morgan Shannon really rocked Winslow. We made a beeline for the nearest java joint so that the big fella could bolster his spirits with a cup of hot bean. The cashier slid the bag with the coffee cups in it toward us. I reached for it, but Winslow got to it first.

"Guess you're paying," he said with a goofy grin.

"How's that fair?"

"You're lead detective, remember? You gotta keep your troops happy." He shrugged. "Besides, I'm sup-porting a family on the meager wages the department pays detectives. You've just got yourself to worry about."

I didn't reply. That stung a little.

Winslow realized what he'd said. "Ah, hell. Sorry, Moccia. I didn't mean—"

I knew he was truly sorry by the tone of his voice and because he addressed me by my family name and not my handle. Still, "You meant what you said. And you were right."

The cashier was staring at us impatiently, so I pulled out some cash and paid him. I turned and walked away as he rang up the sale.

In the car, Winslow reached in and pulled out the paper cups of coffee. He gave each a sniff, and extended one toward me. "A mocha for the Moccia," he tried to joke.

I didn't smile, but I took the coffee, sipped it, and grimaced. It was a far cry from the stuff you get at the high-dollar joints. It was a cup of mud with a pump of generic Bosco.

Winslow chuckled.

I glanced over at him, still a little sour at his comment. Not so much that he said it. More because it was true. "What's so funny, chucklehead?"

He pointed at the paper cup. "Same green design as the ones the Ghost brought to the crime scene. He musta hit the same place on his way over."

I grunted.

"Probably sat in a booth with a coloring book for half an hour, too," Winslow muttered. "Fucking Ghost. Never around when you need him."

I didn't answer. Instead, I started the car, put it

The Last Collar

in gear, and pulled into traffic.

We were silent on the drive to Jessica's parents' house. I tried to mull over what we knew so far about this case, but instead, images of my little Sophia kept popping into my mind. Thank God I had persevered and insisted we name our baby after my grandmother. Sandra wanted to name her Scout because...well she was a star-struck nymphomaniac who probably fell for me because I re-minded her of Bruce Willis and she always saw herself as Demi. She probably fantasized about him every time we...shit, *that* was a crummy thought. But I always felt it was true and maybe that's why we didn't work. I got tired of her fantasy world and she...well, I guess she found another guy who exuded more confidence than I did, and now the three of us were one hot mess, two out-of-lust idiots and a young child who suffered because of us. We were almost to our destination when I realized most of those images in my head came from pictures Sandra had sent me. Not real life memories, but photos, which provided me another sizable dose of self-loathing.

Some kind of father I was.

And sitting next to Winslow, a veritable father of the year candidate on an ongoing basis, didn't exactly help.

Focus, John. Focus on the work.

I pulled to a stop in front of a brownstone. Winslow took a long, loud sip of his coffee and put the cup on the dash. I knew it'd be cold by the time we returned to the car. I also knew he'd drink it anyway.

I opened the door and dumped out my almost full cup of sludge.

"Let's go," I said.

Winslow sighed. "I hate this part."

"Yeah? Well, guess what? You're telling them."

He shook his head. "Uh-uh. You're lead. Your responsibility."

"You're good at it."

"Flattery will get you nowhere, stud."

Normally, I'd keep pleading and flattering, maybe even bribe him a little, and he'd eventually give in and make the notification. But I wasn't in the mood. "Fine. I got it."

Winslow looked mildly surprised but didn't object.

We made our way to the front door and rang the bell. After a few moments, a housekeeper answered. From her expression, I knew immediately that the family had already received the news. How they heard, I didn't know for sure, but I was certain they had. There was no surprise on the housekeeper's face, and her eyes were puffy and red.

"Officers?" she asked, confirming what she already knew.

"Detectives, ma'am," I said. "I'm Detective John Moccia. This is Detective Winslow. May we come in?"

"Of course," she answered. "We've...they've been expecting you."

She led us inside, through a great room, and down a short hallway. She paused at a closed door and glanced at us. "Is it true?" she asked in a whisper. A small, vain hope lighted in her eyes.

"Yes," I said simply.

She nodded, unsurprised, but that flicker of hope dimmed and died. Then she gave a soft knock on the door, twisted the knob, and led us inside.

The room was probably called the library. Shelves of books lined two walls. A barren fireplace took up the far wall. The term that came to mind was grand, not grand as in ostentatious but grand as in exquisitely done. The walls were rich oiled mahogany; the moldings and accents artisan carved. A woman was seated on a small couch, her legs curled up beside her, a glass of wine in her hand. A man sat opposite her in an overstuffed leather chair. The drink in his hand was amber-colored. Scotch, I guessed. He looked like a scotch man to me.

The housekeeper introduced us. "Sir, Madam? It's the police."

Both of them looked our way with obvious reluctance. We all stood awkwardly for a moment. Then I remembered Winslow wasn't going to handle this one.

"Can I offer you a refreshment?" the housekeeper asked in a sad, practiced tone.

"No, thanks," I said. I stepped closer to Mr. and Mrs. Shannon. "I'm Detective John Moccia. This is my partner, Detective Matt Winslow."

They looked at me, then followed my gesture to look at Winslow. He nodded dutifully, and with the perfect blend of somber professionalism.

"I'm sorry to be the one to tell you this," I said, "but I need to talk to you about your daughter, Jessica."

Mr. Shannon's expression remained a mask, but his wife's face seemed to collapse in on itself, contorting as she burst into tears. She lowered her gaze, covering her face with her hands.

"It's true, then," Mr. Shannon said, his voice gruff.

I cleared my throat. "Yes, sir. Jessica is the victim of what we believe to be a homicide. I'm

The Last Collar

sorry for your loss."

He stared back at me, waiting. When I didn't say anything else, he asked, "Is that it?"

I glanced over at Winslow, then back to Mr. Shannon. "Uh..."

"We don't have a lot of details just yet, sir," Winslow stepped in, rescuing me. "And we're still making sense out of what we do know. Once we have something more definitive we'll share it with you."

"But...how? How did it happen?"

"It's best if we don't get into the particulars until we're further along in the investigation," Winslow said smoothly. "But I can tell you that it happened at her apartment, and that early indications are that it was quick. She didn't suffer, sir."

I blinked. I had no idea what "early indications" Winslow was talking about. Plus, given that she was strangled to death, I'd say it *wasn't* quick at all and that she probably suffered plenty.

Mr. Shannon nodded appreciatively, his eyes welling up as he reached for a tissue. "Thank you."

Then I realized what Winslow was doing. His only goal here was to offer some comfort to the parents, and while what he said wasn't technically true, it also wasn't so far out of line with the facts that later on, it wouldn't cause the parents to feel like they'd been lied to.

Mr. Shannon lowered his gaze, wiping at his eyes. His wife sobbed quietly on the couch. Winslow and I stood there, waiting. After about a minute, I asked, "Do you think you'd be up to answering a few questions?"

Mrs. Shannon didn't react, but only kept up with her silent sobs. Her husband glanced up, his eyes wet. He swallowed thickly and gave his head a short shake. "I don't think so, Officer. We...we need a little time."

"Of course," I said immediately. "We can come back tomorrow."

"Our daughter? Where is she?"

"Morgan is with one of our crisis counselors at the moment," I said. "But she's free to leave whenever—"

"No," Mr. Shannon interrupted. "Not her. Jessica."

"Oh." I hesitated, then said, "She'll be available for you to make formal identification at the morgue tomorrow morning. You'll be able to claim the body—uh, claim her by tomorrow evening."

He blinked at me, taking in the information as if it came in a foreign tongue and had to be translated first. His eyes welled up again and he clenched his jaw.

"Until then," Winslow said, "please know that she's being taken care of by the very best people we have."

That seemed to punch through Mr. Shannon's wall, and he nodded to us.

"We'll see ourselves out," I said. "And we'll see you tomorrow, all right?"

"Fine," Mr. Shannon said absently. He raised the glass to his lips and took a long drink.

We left.

In the hallway, the housekeeper appeared immediately at our side. She silently escorted us to the door, then held it open for us. "Thank you," she said, her voice trailing off.

Neither of us replied. Sometimes silence is best.

Back in the car, Winslow started the engine. I glanced over at him. "Well, that sucked."

He reached for his coffee cup on the dashboard. "It always does." He dropped the car into gear, and looked at me expectantly.

"To the barn?" I suggested.

He nodded and sipped his cold coffee before heading out. Then he said, "Might as well get a jump on the paperwork while we wait for some of the forensics to come back."

"The canvass, too."

"That, too."

"Winslow?"

"Yeah."

I looked straight ahead into the darkness, punctuated by the glow of street lamps. "Thanks," was all I said.

Winslow didn't answer. He didn't have to. Like I said, sometimes silence is best.

Chapter Six

"Pretty late," Winslow said. "Want to..."

"Yeah, sure." We'd just left the Shannons' when I glanced at the clock and noticed it was past the big guy's feeding time. If I didn't let him stop off for a bag of cheese-covered cow patties he'd follow me around the station house with his sad brown eyes like a Labrador retriever. "Five Guys?"

"Burgers and fries," he said, finishing my sentence with a big grin on his face. God only knew how he kept his cholesterol in check.

"Listen to you completing my sentences. We've been together so long we've turned into the fucking *Odd Couple*."

"Which one of us is Felix?"

My expression said, *are you for real?* "Two guesses, and I don't own a single goddamn apron." He flipped me the bird as I turned to look out the side window. We were passing through a dicey part of town. Not that our precinct was Fort Apache or anything but we knew a shortcut that took us right by Five Guys on our way to the house and the area wasn't exactly prime real estate—lots of old factory buildings, some of them abandoned. Urban decay was running rampant in the area. "Just don't let Coltrane see you eating that shit. He'll haul you into his office and flush out your rectum with an enema bag."

"Charming," he said with raised eyebrows before redirecting his focus on the road. "Anything jump out at you on this homicide?"

"Not a blessed thing, Matt. I'm a dick not a psychic. You want a prediction, go call Theresa Caputo."

"She doesn't do predictions. She just talks to the dead."

"Well, Jessie Shannon is as dead as they come. I don't see the problem."

"My wife thinks she's great, by the way."

"She knew Jessica Shannon?"

"No, asshole. Theresa Caputo. Sarah paid sixty-five bucks to see her in person."

"I'm sorry she wasted your hard earned—" Some-thing caught my eye. "What the...hey, back up and hang a sharp right."

"Why?" he asked but he had already stopped and was moving the gearshift into reverse. He looked back over his shoulder and mashed the gas pedal. The cheap Detroit-built powertrain whined like a wounded kitten as we hauled ass in reverse.

I unlocked my seatbelt.

"What did you see?"

"Possible two-forty-five."

"Ah shit! Where?"

"Down that alley." It was that particular hour of the day, somewhere between twilight and dark that rendered humans practically blind. It was the body movement more than what I actually saw that drew my focus and told me that an assault was in progress. "Stop!" I flung open the door. "Call it in," I hollered and leapt out of the cruiser.

"John, wait!" he hollered but I was already in pursuit.

Chapter Seven

He had her on her back, legs spread, torn panties on the ground beside her. The victim appeared motionless, but hopefully still alive.

He was unbuckling his belt buckle when he saw me coming. There was just enough ebbing light to see that he was holding a knife in his hand—six inches of serrated terror. Even in the minimal light I could see that he was a stoner. He had that weakness in his eyes that shouldn't be there in the face of panic. His bottom lip hung low revealing blackness where his teeth should've been present. My guess was that he had knocked her out and taken her money before becoming aroused and decided to finish his assault like the macho slug that he was. The crack smokers were all alike; the pilot light in their heads was out but the fire between their legs was inextinguishable.

He turned and ran down the alley, bolting off the starting blocks like Jesse Owens at the Berlin Olympics. *Christ that SOB is fast.* I stopped next to the victim just long enough to see her chest rise and fall.

Winslow was out of the car and barreling down the alley toward us. "Backup is on the way," he yelled.

Jesse Owens was disappearing into the night like the Enterprise after Kirk had given the command to engage the warp engines. The chances of catching the mope were slim. Common sense and protocol told me to stay with the victim. Chasing someone in the dark in this part of town was more than foolish. It was flat out dangerous. I knew that it was wiser let him go.

Nah, fuck that, I said to myself, forcing my legs to pump harder. *Let's give this douchebag a run for his money.*

Winslow was already winded, and falling behind. "John," he called to me, trying to catching his breath. "What the hell?"

My partner was so close to retirement I doubt he'd have considered giving chase on foot but then he didn't have anything to prove, and I did.

Chapter Eight

The color of the perp's clothing didn't help, black jeans and a black tee. Night was quickly falling as I gave hot pursuit. *What the hell?* He appeared to have vanished into thin air. The alley wound around a nesting of old commercial buildings. Security lights should've already come on but they hadn't, or couldn't. I'd spent enough time in the area to know that the bulbs were smashed as soon as they were replaced. In the dark, the alleys were like a rabbit warren, interconnected routes with multiple escape points. Later at night the alleys were filled with dealers and thugs who wouldn't think twice about cornering a cop to liberate his firearm.

I began to understand the magnitude of my stupidity as the night pushed in upon me. A conflict raged within me, a battle between exhilaration and dread, two realities fighting to gain the upper hand.

This is what you want, isn't it, moron?

The Last Collar

The truth was that I was still unsure, and while I was pondering my conflict I lost that edge that keeps a cop safe, and the lights went out.

Chapter Nine

"Fucking idiot!" Winslow swore between ragged breaths.

I kind of heard him and kind of not. I was still out but understood that he was with me, trying to get me to come to. My vision slowly cleared. "Felix," I said, feeling that I was wearing a woozy expression on my face. "Dinner ready?"

"Don't give me that *Odd Couple* shit, asshole! You were knocked unconscious. You could've lost your life. What were you trying to prove?"

I tried to sit up but felt a sharp ache at the base of my skull and winced. "That I'm faster than a crackhead wearing Jordans."

"Not funny. Not fucking funny."

"He was raping her, Matt. What did you want me to do?"

"Stop him. Not chase him through dark alleys with no backup."

"I played the hand I was dealt." I heard the creaking leather and clinking keys of other police officers nearby. "I guess the cavalry has arrived."

"Yeah. Backup is here, you fucking idiot. You want to try to sit up?"

This time I was able to make it up on one elbow. "I'll be okay in a minute. I just need to take it slow."

"Horseshit. You're going to the hospital."

"The fuck I am." I managed to point a finger at him. "Don't you dare embarrass me like that."

"You did it to yourself, John Wayne. I'm just trying to pick up the pieces."

I shook my head, which was a mistake. Clanging bells went off between my ears, and my vision narrowed. "It doesn't fucking matter," I said quietly.

"What the hell is that supposed to mean? It damn well does matter. You take off like a bat out of hell, leaving me to do what? Stay with the victim, like some rookie? I'm sure not keeping up with you running the hundred-yard dash like Flo-Jo."

I had to smile at that, grudgingly. "I don't have the thighs to be Flo-Jo."

"You don't have the brains, either." Winslow scowled at me. "This was stupid, Mocha. No other word for it."

I sat all the way up, feeling a little guilty. I hadn't

looked at it from his perspective when I went barreling down the alley. "Look, it was a once in a lifetime hiccup in judgment and..." I blew out a heavy sigh. "I'm sorry, okay?"

He shook his head woefully. "I know you're headstrong, John, but this...this is too much."

I gave him a sincere look. "I mean it. And as long as the two of us are all right, everything's fine. We are, aren't we?"

There were a couple of lame-ass dicks on the squad who'd lose confidence and bail on their partner at the first sign of undependability or recklessness. History told me that Winslow was not one of those guys.

"Yeah. We're okay...*this* time," he warned.

"Everyone's entitled to one, right?"

He didn't answer my question nor did I expect him to. "Where did he hit you?"

"Back of the head," I answered as I felt the throbbing area.

He lit his flashlight. "Let me have a look." I waited patiently while he examined me, palpating my melon like the doctor his parents probably wanted him to be. "I don't see any blood but you're gonna have one hell of a lump. Could be bleeding inside, or you could have a concussion. Sure you don't want to have it checked out?"

The Last Collar

And have them ask questions about what they'd find? "Nah. Help me up before someone sees us. I'll ice it with a bag of peas when I get home." Winslow helped me to my feet. "We good on our story?"

"What story?"

"You stayed with the victim while I gave brief pursuit, but the perp got away."

"That's what you want me to say?"

"Yeah. That's what I want you to say. And nothing about the knock on the head, either."

"Fine. I guess this means no burgers tonight?"

I shook my head. "Nah. Tomorrow, big guy. Right now, I just want to go home."

Chapter Ten

I knew better. I should've gone straight home but I didn't. My head ached and needed icing, but letting a doper get the drop on me had mortally wounded my ego, and I had this cache of libido that was burning a hole in my pants.

She spotted my car, as I knew she would. Still, I could've simply waved to her and driven off, but I didn't.

Anessa, AKA Dena, AKA Jenny Trix, AKA Lady Lux was a poor man's Beyoncé. She was twenty-five with the face of a fifteen-year-old, which coincidentally was the age at which she had turned her first trick. She was a veritable Lou Gehrig of streetwalkers with an ironman attendance record ten years unmatched—neither rain nor snow kept her from her appointed rounds and she was a hell of a lot more profitable than the United States Postal Service. She patrolled the Bushwick section of Brooklyn three hundred and sixty-some odd days a year. With her long legs and auburn hair extensions she was as iconic a New York landmark as the Empire State Building illuminated red, white and blue on Independence Day. The juxtaposition of the jailbait face and the stripper's body was sheer magic. It constantly caused me to wonder about her net worth, and why she was still shaking her moneymaker for green.

Bushwick. It was where I had made my bones—five long years patrolling DeKalb Avenue from Broadway to Metropolitan. Junkies, pimps, hoes, carjackers, stoolies, and trannies were my extended family, as venerable a group of street trash as any beat cop had ever called kin.

She had a mind like the Dewey Decimal System—every car was catalogued in that pretty head of hers. When it came to identifying a john's car she was better than a Cray supercomputer:

Red Toyota Camry. Ralph the late night fry cook. Quickie BJ. $50.

White BMW 7-Series. Marty the jeweler. Half and half. $100.

She was quicker at identifying johns than the new FBI image analysis platform. She sauntered over to my car without taking her eyes off mine.

The coast looked clear. Nonetheless I quickly glanced down the avenue and then in my rearview mirror, knowing full well that despite my best efforts if the pussy posse was lurking nearby I'd never see them coming. I had that covered of course but I'd have to lie my way out of the solicitation charge. I always carried a cold case hooker photo tucked under the visor in case I needed an alibi.

Have you seen her? Yeah, another hoe slasher. Lady Lux knows every girl on the street. I figured...

It was a plausible lie that no cop would bother to argue with.

"Johnny Mochaccino," she said with a gleam in her eye. "How's my favorite dick?"

I shrugged. "Hard and underpaid."

"No freebies," she warned. "I *know* you're not here wasting *my* time. You've got to pay like all the other curb-crawlers."

"No customer loyalty discount?"

"Uh-uh."

"Detectives Endowment Association?"

It was a negotiation she rarely lost. She shook her head slowly but maintained a huge grin. "Nada!"

"AARP?"

Her grimace read, *Are you for real?*

"I can't get anything on the arm?"

She pursed her lips and lifted her breasts until they billowed out of her low-cut top. "Any more questions?"

Ogling her, I marveled, "God, look at those things. They stand up so straight and tall they practically spit in gravity's eye."

There was usually a current of nervous energy that traveled through me at times like these, but it was gone for some reason. I felt calm, cool, and collected in a way I was unaccustomed to.

"You finished haggling?" she asked with finality.

I nodded.

"The usual?" she asked.

"Uh-huh."

"Well run me over to CVS. I'm fresh out of rubbers."

I placed my hand on her bare arm. "That's all right."

She recoiled with surprise. "Bareback? *You?* Mr. Careful?"

I affirmed with a nod.

"Well, well," she said. "Look who's got some big balls now. 'Course, you know that's gonna cost you more."

"No worries, Lady Lux. I'm on a roll."

Chapter Eleven

When I reached my apartment, the first thing I did was sit down at the kitchen table and press a bag of some frozen peas against the back of my skull. The initial blow hadn't hurt when the crackhead hit me, but it banged loudly when I'd woken up to Winslow. The pain had subsided a little on the ride to drop him off at his house, but later when Lady Lux got me there, I felt like my head was going to explode in equal parts pleasure and pain. It was the strangest sexual experience I'd had in a while, and I still wasn't sure if I loved it or hated it. All I knew was that it made me glad to be alive.

Don't get too used to that, sport.

The frozen bag of peas worked wonders. The pain subsided to a dull throb inside of five minutes. Still holding the bag to my head, I got up and walked into the bedroom. I kicked off my boots and slid off my jeans. Aided by the weight of my gun on the belt they dropped to the carpet with a thud. I pulled the peas away to take off my shirt, and even in that short amount of time, felt the difference. I pressed the bag back up against my scalp.

Winslow was right. I probably had a concussion, or worse, a subdural hematoma or something. Bleeding on the brain was not exactly something two aspirin would handle.

But I found that I didn't really care, and if I didn't wake up in the morning, who else would really give a shit? Winslow, maybe.

I wanted to sleep, but I wasn't sure if I should. I'd always heard you shouldn't let people with head injuries go to sleep, and I believed it. Winslow told me once that it was an old wives' tale, but I didn't buy that. Once, when I was a kid, I went outside with wet hair after a shower. My dad said never to do that because I'd catch cold, but I didn't believe him. I ended up with a case of strep throat that was an ass-kicker. He never said I-told-you-so, but when he told me I needed to always keep my neck warm after that, I listened to him. That's why most of my shirts are some version of a turtleneck design.

They say we should believe in science, and I guess I'm okay with that. But old wives have been around longer than science, and I figure they know their shit. Old men, too.

So I decided to stay awake for a couple of hours, just to be safe.

There was nothing on TV except the replay of the Rangers game, and I'd already heard the score on the radio on our way for coffee earlier, so I flipped past it. Infomercials, old, bad movies, and syndicated sitcoms made up most of my options.

I ended up back on the hockey game. Maybe there'd be a fight or something to make up for the fact that I knew they were destined to lose to the goddamn Islanders.

The second period ended in boring fashion, and I dozed in my chair during the intermission. When my phone rang, the shrill sound surprised me. I stumbled out of the chair and toward the kitchen. An old landline hung on the wall. I had a cell phone, so I hardly ever used the house phone, but department regs required us to have a landline. Plus, my folks liked to call me on it instead of the cell. I'd never understood why.

"Yeah?" I answered, my voice thick.

"Are you drunk?" came a woman's voice.

For a split second, I thought it was my mother. Then a moment later, I wondered if it was Lady Lux, getting off work and wanting to go a second round. Maybe even on the house. But as the sleep cleared, I realized it was neither of them.

"No, Sandra. But I wish I was."

She didn't know how to answer that, so she did what she always did. She ignored it. "Why do you even carry a cell phone if you don't ever answer it?"

"Huh?"

"I've been calling you all day. I've left you, like, six messages."

"Hold on." I put the phone down and hunted around for my cell. I found it in the pocket of my jeans. The battery was dead.

Back in the kitchen, I picked up the phone again. "Sorry," I said. "Battery died."

"You don't own a charger?" Her tone was impatient and accusing.

"I was on a case." And I was with Winslow, who was pretty much the only person I worried about being able to get in touch with me when we weren't together.

"Of course. Something *important*."

"It was a dead girl, Sandy. You know, a homicide?"

"Don't call me that. My name's Sandra. And I know what you do for a living, John. Christ, I *know*."

My head throbbed. I looked forlornly for the bag of peas. It was nestled on the headrest of my chair. "Do you have any idea what time it is?"

"Ten o'clock."

"Your time. That means it's one o'clock here."

"I don't care. If you'd answered your phone when I called you at three, we wouldn't be talking now."

And how nice that would be. "What do you want, Sandra?" I used the preferred version of her name as a peace offering.

It didn't work. "How about you pulling even a fraction of your weight as a father? That'd be a nice start."

I didn't want to rehash my shortcoming as a dad with her right now. "Specifically, what?"

"You're late with the child support. Again."

I glanced down at my cell to check the date, then remembered it was dead. "What's the date?"

"The fourth, John. It's supposed to be here on the first. In fact, I count on it to be here on the first. So I can pay for things like rent and food for our daughter. Things you don't seem to give half a shit about."

I started to say I was sorry, but her tone pissed me off. "Look—"

"No, you look. All you have to do is set up an automatic transfer with your bank. It takes five minutes. Then we don't have to have this conversation every month."

"I don't trust that automatic stuff. Not with money."

"That's ridiculous."

"I've seen too much fraud."

"Don't try to use your job to justify your superstition. You work dead bodies, John. Not fraud."

"I still see plenty of fraud."

"Not from Chase."

"They're the biggest crooks around."

"Spare me. Are you going to wire me the money in the morning, or do I need to call my lawyer?"

"Is your lawyer here or out there in San Diego?"

"What does it matter? Unlike you, he's not afraid of technology. Now what's it to be?"

I let out a resigned sigh. "I'll wire you the fucking money."

"Gee, thanks. You're swell. By the way, you might want to include a little something extra while you're at it."

"Why?"

"Really?"

"Yeah, really. Why?"

"Because Sophia's birthday is later this month. It'd be nice for her to have a nice new dress for her fourth birthday, don't you think?"

I couldn't answer that. I had something caught in my throat.

Sandra took my silence as insolence. "Or not. I'll figure it out, just like I always do. Goodbye, John, you piece of shit."

"Wait!"

There was a moment of silence, but no dial tone followed. Finally, she asked, "What?"

I swallowed, and wet my lips. "I...I want to see her for her birthday."

"Do you really think that's a good idea? She barely knows who you are."

"Yeah, well, I'm not the one who moved way the fuck out to San Diego. That has a little to do with me being unable to see her."

"Because you spent so much time with her those first two years in New York, huh?"

I didn't reply. Her words stung, because they were true.

"I could barely get you to spend one weekend a month with her, and even those got cut short. So don't cry me a river now."

"I...I was working, and..."

"Yeah, John, I know. The job. It's always the fucking job. Well, that's what you wanted, and that's what you got, and now your little girl barely knows you exist, so I hope you're happy. Now wire me the money in the morning or I'll have you served with papers and my lawyer will garnish your wages."

"Sandy..."

"Fuck off."

This time the click and the dial tone were unmistakable. I hung up the receiver and staggered back into the living room. I stared at the chair and the peas for a few long moments, then went into the bedroom instead. I crashed down onto the mattress and let sleep take me. Hell, maybe it'd take me forever, if I had any luck at all.

Chapter Twelve

"Well, princess, you look like shit." Winslow's voice was light-hearted but his expression had a hint of worry to it. "Did you sleep at all last night?"

I plopped a bag of coffees onto my desk, and reached in to fish out his straight black. "Got my requisite four hours. You?"

"Got home too late to bust one off with the old lady, so I tossed and turned."

I handed him his coffee. "As in, you tossed one off and turned over to go to sleep?"

He smiled, the mirth touching his eyes. "Damn. We've been married too long, Mocha."

"You and Sarah? Or you and me?"

"Yes," Winslow said. He sipped his coffee, glancing toward the back of my head and raising his eyebrows in a subtle question.

"Not even a headache," I lied. I pulled my café mocha out of the bag and tossed the bag in the trash. "Back to the Shannons' place for follow up?"

"Uh, yeah, but..."

"What?"

Winslow took a sip of his coffee, stalling.

"What, Matt?"

He sighed. "El Tee wants to see us."

I blinked. "Fuck."

"Yeah."

"Where's the Ghost? We should bring him in with us." A sergeant was supposed to provide some cover for his troops, but that was a lot to hope for with Gastineau.

"Where do you think he is?"

"In the fucking wind," I said. "As usual."

Winslow spread his hands in a there-you-go gesture.

"Fuck," I repeated. Then I put my untouched mocha down on my desk. "Well, let's get it over with."

We wended our way through the bullpen. Most of the other detectives ignored us, going about their business. A couple gave a distracted nod while typing or talking on the phone. But I caught a sidelong glance or two as well.

"What's up?" I asked Winslow.

He shrugged. "I know what you know."

"When'd you get here this morning? Sarah drop

you off?"

"No, I took the train. So about seven. Why?"

"And who told you Coltrane wanted to see us?"

"Eva. Why?"

Eva Muramatsu was technically Coltrane's secretary, but the truth was she handled most of the unit's needs. She was the daughter of a Japanese father and a Puerto Rican mother, and even though she was well into her fifties, she still looked thirty-five. It wasn't her looks that kept this place glued together, though. It was her mind, and her organization skills. Coltrane might command the unit, but his secretary kept it running. Nothing escaped her notice.

"Think about it," I said to Winslow, keeping my voice low. "If Coltrane just wanted to yell at us, he'd have come barreling through the bullpen himself, bellowing out orders. But he didn't. He sent Eva with a message instead."

"So?"

"So, sending Eva is more subtle. It means he's not going to yell at us."

He thought about that for a moment. "Yeah, that makes sense. So what is it?"

"I don't know." I didn't have to add that I didn't like it, either.

Eva was talking on the phone and typing

something at the same time when we approached. Coltrane's door was closed and the shades drawn. She made eye contact with me, gave me a motherly smile, and jerked her head toward the office behind her.

Go on in, she mouthed, never breaking stride as her manicured nails clicked on the keyboard nor interrupting her conversation on the phone.

The black stenciled letters LIEUTENANT MARCUS COLTRANE stood out on the frosted glass door panel. I raised my hand and rapped my knuckles on it three times.

"Come!" Coltrane barked.

I opened the door and entered. Winslow followed me in. Apparently I was taking lead on this little meeting. I made a mental note that my so-called partner was going to be buying me lunch later if this turned out to be an ass-chewing after all.

Coltrane looked up from the paperwork he was reading. "Close the door," he directed Winslow.

I started to sit in one of the chairs in front of Coltrane's desk.

"Don't bother," he snapped at me. "You won't be here long enough to warm the seat."

I stood tall, waiting for Winslow to join me. Maybe I'd been wrong about him sending Eva.

This was definitely shaping up as a potential yell-fest.

Coltrane gave me his very best boss mean-mug. Even though I'd been on the receiving end of it before, it was still a little unnerving. I shifted involuntarily from one foot to the other. It irritated me that Coltrane could just stare and make me feel that way, but there it was all the same. Nothing I could do about it. Sure, the guy was an asshole, but he was a *scary* asshole.

Finally, he said, "You look like shit, Mocha."

"Second time today I've been advised of that, sir."

"I'm you, I'd get used to hearing it all day. Why don't you try coming to work looking like a professional instead of a substitute teacher?"

My face burned a little. Winslow let out a small, nervous titter.

Coltrane turned his eyes toward my partner. "You're no better, fat ass. You dress like a first-year real estate agent."

Winslow laughed weakly. "Heh. Well, I do have a great loft apartment available in Flatbush that I can show you, boss. Just came on the market."

Coltrane didn't laugh. He stared. Most of the air left the room. I shifted my feet again, and sensed Winslow doing the same.

The Last Collar

Get to it, I thought. Jesus, I hated how he liked to make people squirm. More than that, I hated how he was able to make people squirm. A small tinder of anger started smoldering in my chest.

After what seemed like forty minutes, Coltrane sniffed derisively and leaned back in his chair, folding his hands at his chest. "I'm told you two made a trip to the Shannon residence last night."

I nodded. "We made notification, and attempted a first interview."

Coltrane stared at me.

"They already knew," I continued. "And we put off the interviews until this morning."

"They were grieving," Winslow added.

"No shit." Coltrane sat still, considering us both. Then he said, "I guess I can't expect a couple of chuckle-heads like you to be aware of anything that isn't right smack in front of you, so it doesn't surprise me that you don't know who the fuck this Shannon guy is."

"He's rich?" I offered.

"Again, no shit. He's also an at-large member of CPAC."

Winslow and I exchanged a glance. From his expression, I knew he didn't have a clue what CPAC was, either.

Coltrane caught the look. "Christ, you really are

a couple of stumbling fools, huh? CPAC. The Citizen's Police Advisory Committee?"

I shook my head slightly and gave Coltrane a lame half-shrug. "So they have coffee and donuts with the brass once a month, or..."

"Can it, Mocha. Are you really that unaware?"

"I guess so."

Coltrane sighed in disgust. "Well, I don't have time for a civics lesson *or* a history lesson. Let me put it to you this way. This committee *does* have coffee and donuts with not just the brass, but the *executive* brass. That includes the Chief of Police. And he pays attention to what they say during those little coffee klatches. Get it?"

"Why haven't I heard of them?" I asked.

"Probably because you're an ignorant fucking moron," Coltrane snapped. Then, with seeming reluctance, he added, "And they're a low-profile advisory group. The Chief and his commanders use them as barometers of the community. They're an official group but don't have official power. But you better believe they have referent power."

I wasn't sure what referent power was exactly, but I got the gist of the situation. "So is this the part where you tell us we can get whatever we need to work this important case?"

Coltrane scowled. "This is the part where I tell

you in no uncertain terms, do *not* fuck this up. Find the guy who did this, and fast. People are watching this one. Important people."

I didn't answer. I waited for the other shoe to drop. I guessed he was going to reassign the case to someone safer and more politically sensitive. Maybe to Detectives Vanilla and Milquetoast or whatever.

Instead, he said, "And yeah, whatever you need to move this along, you get."

That surprised me a little, but I took it in stride. "Does that include getting our DNA and other forensics moved to the front of the line?"

Coltrane fixed me with a withering glare. "I already did that, brainiac. You got any other requests, put them through Eva. I'll see you here at five o'clock for an up-date so I can give one to command at five-thirty. Have something for me."

I nodded. Winslow murmured something to indicate that he understood as well. Since Coltrane's last order was also clearly a dismissal, I turned on my heels and exited the office.

Walking past Eva, I gave her a wave and a confident wink that I wasn't sure I felt. Winslow hurried behind me. As soon as we were clear of her desk and around a corner, he stopped and leaned his back against the wall.

"Shiiii-iiit, Mocha," he whispered heavily.

I stopped, waiting for him to say his piece.

"This is some high jingo," he said.

"The hell? High jingo?"

"Politics, man. High and hard politics."

"Yeah, I know what we're dealing with. But I never heard of high jingo before."

Winslow shrugged. "They say it in L.A."

"Oh. Well, wrong coast, Kojak."

Winslow shrugged. "This is some heavy shit, Mocha. We've got to step lightly. And move fast."

"Yeah, I was just at the same meeting you were, remember?"

"I'm not kidding." He tapped the badge on his belt. "I'm seven months out from my twenty-five. Seven months. This can't go off the rails for me, you under-stand? I've got Sarah and the kids to think about. Shit, I've got *myself* to think about."

"You want off the case? Ask."

He shook his head. "No. We're partners, and you know I'll stick. What I'm saying is we gotta listen to the El Tee on this one. We do things by the book. We're careful."

"Fine with me."

"And we put in the hours until we can collar up."

"You're the one always bitching if you don't get

off by four-thirty."

"I'm goddamn serious, Mocha. We fly hard and straight. Otherwise, it's going to be us that gets jammed up, instead of some mope who did the deed."

I raised my hands in surrender. "All right. Now, are we going to get back to work, or just talk about it?"

Winslow stared at me for a long moment. "I'm fucking begging you here, Mocha. You get that?"

"I got it."

"Yeah, huh?" He didn't sound sure.

"I got it," I repeated with more emphasis.

Winslow continued to look at me, his eyes searching. Then, after a moment longer, he seemed satisfied. "Okay. Let's go, then."

We headed back toward our desks. The coffees were probably cold, but I wanted to make a couple of calls before we headed out. Mostly, I wanted to see if Coltrane's push on our forensics had done any good.

"High jingo," I mused aloud as we walked. "Where'd you pick that up? You get it from some L.A. cops at a conference or something?"

Winslow shrugged. "Nah. It was in a Michael Connelly novel."

"You read?" I raised my eyebrows in surprise.

I'd always had Winslow figured for a can of beer in front of the TV kind of guy.

"Sarah bought me the book for my birthday."

"So you *had* to read it."

"Yep."

"Cop book?"

"Detective book, yeah."

"Sort of a busman's holiday, ain't it? Reading books like that?"

"I didn't pick it," Winslow said. "But I plowed through it twenty minutes a night in bed right before lights out."

That was smart. "With Sarah strategically seated right next to you. Well played, my partner."

He shook his head mournfully. "Not really. She thought I enjoyed it so much that now all my presents are books. I get 'em for no special occasion sometimes."

I smiled. In spite of everything—the job, my head, my ex, Coltrane, even the jackpot of a case we were stuck in the middle of—the thought of Winslow mired knee-deep reading books he didn't want to made me laugh deep down in my belly.

"It ain't funny," Winslow groused.

"Well, it ain't high jingo, either," I said. "So that's something."

Chapter Thirteen

My calls to Forensics confirmed what Coltrane told us. We'd have results on some of the workups by late morning or early afternoon. I put the phone back on the receiver, impressed.

When I told Winslow, it actually made him smile. "Good news. Maybe we'll catch a ground ball off the DNA."

"Maybe," I said, but I wasn't too sure. "For now, let's head over to see the Shannons."

"If we must."

"Well, listen to you with the tragic, 'If we must.' Look who isn't bright-eyed and bushy-tailed this morning."

A sharp pain reared its ugly head behind my right eye causing it to close and my face to contort. I didn't know if it was a residual symptom of getting clobbered the night before or if it was something worse. I was really hoping it wasn't something worse. "You ever have one of those days when the job just plain wears you out?"

"All the time. This one of those days, my brave little buckaroo?"

"Yeah, it's *one* of them." I rubbed my temple in a circular motion hoping the pain would disappear but it didn't.

"You all right?"

"I don't know," I said unhappily, continuing to squeeze my eye shut against the pain. "I'm all fucked up today. Maybe my sinuses are acting up."

"I've got Sudafed in my drawer."

"No, that's okay. They make me sleepy. Let's hit the road. Maybe it'll stop when I hit the fresh air."

"I guess those turtlenecks of yours don't ward off everything."

"They certainly don't ward off irritating partners."

Winslow wrinkled his brow and flipped me the bird, after which I followed him out to the car for the ride over to the home of Mr. and Mrs. Moneybags.

The ride to their home was uneventful, tranquil even. I think that Winslow was still inwardly pissed because I hadn't just rolled over when he appealed to me to fly straight and true on our "high jingo" case, the one all the brass were watching. In any event he clammed up pretty tightly and I have to say that I enjoyed the peace and quiet.

Turned out the Shannons did have first names. They were Martin and Elizabeth but it wasn't hard to see that we weren't supposed to use them, not lowly civil servants like us. They were to be addressed only as Mr. and Mrs. Shannon and in no other manner. I mean, Christ, to them we were on a plane with the hired help. You had to wonder how people make that kind of money. I'm talking about fuck-you-money, the kind of money that buys unconditional arrogance and entitlement, the kind we all play the lottery in the hope of winning.

Although...even Jessica Shannon played the lottery. *Huh,* I started to think. Maybe she craved her own financial independence. Maybe being beholden to Mommy and Daddy Moneybags wasn't her cup of tea... or not. It was a less than half-baked idea I didn't bother to share with Winslow.

Despite all their wealth, Morgan and her well-heeled parents looked like shit as we were once again shown into the library. I would've been surprised if they didn't. I mean, after the early morning visit to the morgue and seeing...Christ, the thought of it even got me choked up and my heart skipped a couple of beats. I couldn't imagine how they felt after seeing their little girl, their pretty little shining star, lying cold, pale, and lifeless on a morgue autopsy table. I know a sight like that certainly would've taken the wind out of my sails. They had no doubt showered and dressed but they did have that put-together look. Mr. Shannon's slacks lacked that razor sharp crease I had seen on our first visit and Mrs. Shannon's suit looked, well...rumpled. It was as if the angst they were experiencing had spread throughout their bodies and permeated the fabric of their clothing, making them appear lifeless. Garb aside, their faces told it all—they were colorless and haggard, their eyes glassy and strained, three morbid pictures that in sum were worth thousands of dreadful words.

Winslow and I were standing around like a couple of pathetic lummoxes when Mr. Shannon snapped, "Well, sit down already."

We did as instructed.

Morgan apologized for her father by conveying a sad smile.

The housekeeper brought us coffee without asking.

I'm the lead. I guess I'd better open my mouth. "Detective Winslow and I know that this is a very difficult time for you but it's essential that we talk with you now so that we identify all possible

The Last Collar

parties of interest and chart our investigation efficiently." I glanced quickly at Winslow. He seemed to be impressed with my professional demeanor. *This is all for you, big guy.*

It was obvious that Mrs. Shannon was fighting to hold back her tears.

"Morgan told us that Jessica had recently been in a relationship with a gentleman named Arturo Calderas. Did either of you meet him?"

Mr. Shannon seemed shocked, upset actually. News of the relationship had quite obviously startled him and not in a good way. He turned to Morgan. "Who the hell is this Arturo character? Jessica never mentioned him to me. Not once."

"He was her boyfriend, *Daddy.*"

The hell? There was something about the way she said "Daddy" that bothered me. It was almost flirty. I pondered her inflection for a moment until Martin shook his head unhappily and barked, "What kind of guy was he?" His head ratcheted toward his wife. "Did you know?" he asked accusatorily.

"Just in passing," she replied timidly. "Jessica mentioned him a few times but it didn't sound like any-thing serious."

He slapped his legs just above the knees with both hands, his expression showing extreme frustration, before turning to us. "There, you see? They tell me nothing." He mumbled, "Son of a bitch," and scowled at his wife briefly before turning to Morgan. "Well, what the hell do we know about him?" he demanded angrily.

"They dated about six months, Dad. He's an artist."

"Someone of note," Mr. Shannon asked in a high-handed manner, "or another penniless nobody?"

Shannon replied with irritation, "I don't know, Daddy. You think every artist is a nobody." She said "Daddy" properly this time, with a hint of irritation.

"That's because most of them are," he insisted.

"Do you know if his work was financially self-sustaining?" I asked to settle the squabble. "In plain English, did he earn a living at it?"

Morgan shrugged. "I think so but I don't know. Jessica never mentioned how well he did. If you're asking if I think he enjoyed having a wealthy girlfriend, I already told you the answer is yes. Jessie grabbed the check whenever the three of us were out together and he wasn't shy with his ordering. He always asked for Patron in his margaritas. He wasn't much for pasta. He ordered steak and seafood off the menu."

"Tequila," Mr. Shannon bristled. "The Latin's drink," he commented with indignation and signaled to the housekeeper as if he were beckoning to a bartender. She turned and walked to the bar. "Well where can I find this *artiste*? I'd like to have a talk with him."

"Sir, if you don't mind, it's better if we handle the interviews," Winslow said.

He seared Winslow with an arrogant gaze before diverting his eyes and acquiescing. "Yes, all right. For now." The housekeeper handed him his scotch. He took a sip, then turned to his wife. "You know, I'm really angry. Would it have been such a big goddamn deal for you to tell me that Jessica was seeing someone? I mean, what's the big secret?"

"It was just something she mentioned in passing. You know, girl talk," Mrs. Shannon answered. "I certainly would've told you if it sounded like they were getting serious."

"Do you think our daughter's death is serious enough?" he sniped.

His wife misted up and grabbed a tissue.

"Back off, Dad," Morgan pleaded.

Winslow and I exchanged knowing glances. We just loved it when the interviewees did all the work for us.

"I will *not*," he snapped back and gulped the rest of his scotch.

"You want to know why no one tells you anything? It's because you turned piranha on every guy Jessie or I ever brought home. Who wants to hear your shit? 'He's the wrong race. He's too short. He's in the wrong profession. He slouches. He burps. He farts. His teeth are yellow.' I mean *my God*, no one has ever been good enough for you."

"Watch your tone, young lady. Don't forget for a minute whom you're talking to."

"Trust me. I know exactly *whom* I'm talking to."

"Folks," I interjected. "Emotions are running high and it's understandable, but it would be better if we all tried to calm down a little."

"Was it wrong of me to want the best for my girls?" he asked heatedly, paying no regard to my request.

"I've got news for you, *Father*. Prince William is already is spoken for and Prince Harry is getting all the tail he can handle."

"Oh cut the bluster, Morgan. No one asked you to bring home the goddamn Duke of Cambridge. How is a father supposed to react when his daughter dates bikers, tattoo artists, and other assorted lowlifes?"

"Lowlifes?" she exploded. "So it wasn't the men both of your daughters dated, it was just the ones *I* dated. Well, what about *Lenny*? He turned out to be a real beauty, didn't he?"

I motioned to Winslow to see which of us was going to ask. His return gaze said, "Sorry, dude, you're the lead." I cleared my throat loudly. "Who's Lenny?"

"Damn it!" Mr. Shannon slammed his empty glass down on the coffee table and stood up. "I knew that weasel's name would pop up sooner or later." He started for the door.

"Uh, Mr. Shannon, the interview's not over, sir."

"The *hell* it's not," he said hotly, not looking back as he left the room.

Those remaining in the room looked at one another, still startled by Mr. Shannon's abrupt exit. The question on everyone's mind was, *what do we do now?*

"Shall we continue without your husband?" I asked.

Mrs. Shannon thought for a long moment before replying, "I don't think he'd like that. He'll be upset about being left out of the conversation."

"And he'll howl at us and call us incompetents

for providing an inadequate accounting of what he missed," Morgan said, apparently still hot.

"Then I guess we'll come back," Winslow said. He was the one who was so hot to solve the case so if he was already on his feet...

What the hell am I waiting for?

"I'll see you to the door," Morgan offered. The look in her eye told me that she had something to tell us in confidence. We said goodbye to Mrs. Shannon and made our way to the door.

As I surmised, Morgan followed us out onto the front porch and closed the door behind her to ensure privacy. Just then three large landscaping trucks pulled up and enough Latino groundskeepers got out to trim and manicure an eighteen-hole golf course.

"Get many like my dad?" she asked as she lit a cigarette and took a long drag.

"Oh, you'd be surprised," Winslow replied.

"I guess he's running a D-minus in his anger management classes," I quipped.

"Ya think?" she said, a long-overdue smirk finally surfacing on her tired face.

"What's your old man do?"

"You mean aside from eating cops for lunch?"

"Yeah."

"He eats cops for lunch professionally," she

replied most matter-of-factly. "He's a criminal defense attorney."

One more knowing exchange between Winslow and me. *Jesus. How fucking ironic. The haughty douchebag made his fortune defending murdering scumbags and now...shit, I'll bet this really sticks in his goddamn craw.* "Hence the obvious lack of respect for Detective Winslow and myself."

"Hence."

In his role as defense counsel, Martin Shannon was undoubtedly used to routinely disemboweling law enforcement officers on the witness stand. *It's probably killing him to have to answer our questions instead of cross-examining us.* "So I'm guessing that you have something to tell us that you didn't want your parents to hear. Does it have anything to do with this Lenny character?"

"Uh-huh. They were married."

"I'm gonna go out on a limb and say that their marriage didn't go very well."

"One and done," Morgan replied.

"Their marriage only lasted *one* year?" Winslow asked with surprise.

"Thirteen months to be exact. I guess there's a reason it's the most unlucky number of all."

At least they made it to the wedding alter. Sandra and I were going at it like cats and dogs before the end of her first trimester. "Why the divorce?"

She cautiously looked around despite the fact that we were alone and the landscaper's lawnmowers had started up, producing enough noise to drown out a 747 on final approach. "My parents *think* they're divorced, but..."

Okay, here it comes and I'll bet it's a beauty.

"I'm sure you'd find out on your own so I'm not really talking out of school." She sighed wearily. "They're not divorced. Lenny's in jail."

My head bounced up and down in a knucklehead-ish manner. "Finding out that he's in the slammer? Yeah, I think we'd have been able to figure that one out."

"What did he do?" Winslow asked.

Morgan stared at the ground while she spoke. "He slept with one of his patients and she was..." She took a moment to clear her throat. "Sixteen years old."

Whoa! I wasn't expecting that bombshell. "He was a physician?"

"A psychologist. I mean, in Lenny's defense the girl was a slutty little nymphomaniac with a body like Kate Upton."

"Okay, so the girl was heavy-duty jailbait. Still, I'm surprised that he was convicted on statutory rape. I mean your father, the hot shot cop-destroying-attorney couldn't get him off on that?" *That is if he's actually as good as he believes he is.*

"He doesn't know, neither of them do. They think he ran off with another woman. Neither Jessie or I thought they'd be able to deal with the shame, and with my dad's holier than thou attitude...so we wrote him out of the script, so to speak."

"And you've been keeping Jessica's tawdry little secret all this time?" Winslow asked.

She nodded, her eyes once again focused on the ground. "What kind of question is that? Of course I kept quiet. She's my sister."

A weed whacker kicked up a pebble and it hit one of the windows. We all heard the *ting*, as it ricocheted off the glass. The blinds flew upward and Jaws appeared at the window looking for a gardener to devour. It didn't take long for him to notice his least favorite daughter and the two interlopers holding court in front of his estate. He seared us with his eyes and disappeared from the window. He was undoubtedly coming for us.

Stalwart soldiers that we were, we decided that retreat was the best option.

"Thanks for your help," I said, holding my hand out to Morgan. She took it. Her grip was firm, and

I could almost feel grief coursing through her skin. She held my hand for a long moment before letting go.

"Find him," she whispered. "Find my sister's killer."

I nodded slowly. "We'll do our best. I promise."

Then we got the hell out of there.

Chapter Fourteen

"That could have gone better," Winslow said once we were in the car.

"Could've gone worse, too."

"How? If mister criminal defense attorney, hot shot advisor to the chief had torn actual flesh from our bones?"

"That would have been worse, yeah."

Winslow sighed. "Let's stop for lunch."

"It's ten o'clock."

"I need a cheeseburger."

"You need a cheeseburger like Britney Spears needs a bad relationship."

"Don't mess with me on this, Mocha. I'm hungry. I need a cheeseburger. Now."

I shook my head sadly. "You eat like that all the time, you're going to last about six months into retirement before your heart bursts."

"Nice. Shut up and find a fucking White Castle."

We settled for a diner. I got coffee and toast.

Winslow had a double cheeseburger. In between bites, he said, "Hey, at least the sister gave with the ex-husband, right?"

"Husband."

"What?"

"Husband. He's not an ex," I reminded him. "They're still married."

He glared at me and took another bite. "You know what I mean," he said while chewing.

"That's disgusting. Chew with your mouth closed."

He didn't.

I turned away and reached for my coffee.

Winslow ate in silence for a little while. Then he asked, "How's your head?"

"Better."

"You take an aspirin for it?"

"No, I got out of Martin Shannon's earshot."

Winslow chuckled, but his heart wasn't in it. "Yeah, that'll do it. Typical rich prick."

"Typical defense attorney."

"Typical cocksucker."

"Don't knock cocksuckers," I said. "They perform an essential service."

"I wouldn't know. I've been married too long."

About thirty snappy comebacks flitted through my head, but I let them pass. The truth was, my head still ached, and I was getting weary of all the banter. Some days, it felt good, like a favorite song or something. Other days, it felt like work.

"You figure that was the real him, or just an act?" I asked.

Winslow's chewing slowed. "Who, Shannon? Oh, that's gotta be him."

"Yeah?"

"Yeah. You don't think so?"

"I don't know. But either way, we left that interview with jack shit outside of Lenny."

"The old man didn't know about Arturo the artist. We got that."

"Pardon me. A bonanza."

"It's something."

"It's crap. What happened was a rich, criminal defense attorney limited our questions and put us on the defensive."

"You think he's hiding something?"

"Everyone's hiding something. I just don't know if it has to do with the case, or if he just did it out of habit."

"Maybe he's really upset. He looked like hell."

"I'm sure he is upset. I felt for him and the mother the first moment I saw them. But then he went into his routine and—"

"I don't think it was a routine."

I shrugged. "Either way, the box score says we got what? Arturo was a surprise to no one except Dad, and Jessica Shannon used to be married to a guy who's now doing time."

"I don't know what else we could've gotten from them, Mocha. There's a lot of grief in that family right now."

I thought about that. "I'm guessing there was plenty of grief before Jessica was killed. But you're right, we did get something else. Jessica was clearly Daddy's favorite."

"And that helps us how?"

"I don't know. But it's good to know."

"So are the Chinese zodiac signs, but it don't exactly move our case forward. And in case you forgot, Coltrane was pretty clear about us making that happen. Like yesterday."

I tipped my chin toward his plate. "You're the one who needed to eat two hours after breakfast."

"I'm serious."

"I know. But so am I. You know as well as I do that you never know what the important fact in a case might be."

"Daddy's favorite little girl married a scumbag? That's going to crack the case?"

"Probably not, but you get my drift. You ready?"

Winslow stuffed the last of his burger into his mouth and nodded. "Les guh," he grunted at me.

"Huh?"

He swallowed, and almost choked. Then he said, "Let's go."

We rode in silence to the station, each of us thinking about the case. It was another of our partner rituals. Jabber about the case, argue about it, then quiet reflection. I don't know if it helped, or if it worked at all, but our clearance rate spoke for itself.

A murder at home was usually one of two things. A robbery gone bad or a passion killing. Since we'd ruled out robbery that left us with passion. It was possible that Jessica had some love-from-afar stalker who could have done this. She was attractive enough and seemed to be out in the world enough for that to happen. But the odds were that it was someone she knew. And the heavy odds right now were on Arturo.

I ran the case through my head a couple more times as I drove. The pulsing headache made it difficult to think, but I pushed through it. I tried to envision other scenarios, letting my imagination wander.

As was our habit, talk resumed as we neared the station.

"I'm thinking Arturo is first up," Winslow said.

"Gotta be," I agreed.

"What else could it be?"

"Strange-o stalker?"

"Sure, I suppose. Long odds, though."

"Maybe being Daddy's favorite carried some fringe benefits."

Winslow cringed and chuckled at the same time. "You're evil."

"It happens. Not just in poor families, and did you catch the way Morgan called old Marty, 'Daddy?'"

"No. Why?"

"Really? It was like phone sex. It got me hard."

Winslow gave it a minute to sink in. "Guess I missed it."

"Man, you happily married guys are lame."

He shrugged, then segued, "So, what? He got jealous of Arturo? He never even knew about him until this morning."

"Who knows? I'm just saying, it's a possibility."

"So's a green sky, but I ain't layin' any cash on that, either."

I remained silent. Then, "Maybe it's someone we haven't come across yet. A door man or something?"

Winslow considered. "It's happened before."

"Or someone from one of her charity groups?"

"Always a possibility."

"Maybe she's something of a tease. Some whack job didn't take kindly to getting led on, followed her home?"

"All stuff we'll have to run down," Winslow said. "*After* we look into Arturo. And roust him."

"Yeah." For all my brain-storming, Arturo was still the most likely candidate.

When we got to the station, we went straight to our desks in the bullpen. "I got Arturo," I said. "You run down anything else that strikes you as interesting."

"Like what? Your door man theory?"

"Like was Lenny really popped for statch rape or was it something else? Like who has Daddy defended lately? Like who do we need to contact to get membership lists to all of her favorite charities? Christ, you need me to hold your hand? Is this the first day of school or something?"

Winslow held up his palms. "Okay, okay. Easy, big guy." Then he snickered a little.

"What?"

"It's just hard seeing you get so worked up when you look like a beatnik poet waiting his turn for open mike night."

I touched the turtleneck. The beatnik reference

was his go to. Calling me European ran a close second. I used to point out that Steve McQueen wore a turtleneck, but it didn't matter. All I got in return were foreskin jokes.

"Run the checks," I told him, not biting.

I sat down at the computer and got to work on Arturo.

Arturo Calderas. Twenty-nine years old. Listed alternatively as Hispanic or white, depending on which report you read. Sealed juvenile record containing three items. I'd need to get Coltrane to grease the wheels to get access to those. He showed eleven different addresses since his first entry, which was one of the sealed files. He was fifteen at the time. Two more juvenile entries, then eight more in his adult jacket.

I pored through each entry, calling up the original report. The first seven were poor quality scanned files of the original handwritten report. Arturo took two misdemeanor falls for prostitution and five for petty theft. All of them happened between the ages of eighteen and twenty-two. The reports all read the same. Young Arturo was ripping off his johns, got caught twice for servicing them too. Charges dropped in all of the theft cases at the request of the victim.

No surprise there. Court records were public

records. I doubt most of those johns cared to have what they were doing with Arturo immortalized for any and all to see. Odds were, since he got caught and charged initially, the john got back some or most of whatever Arturo stole and was willing to call it good.

One soliciting charge was dropped for lack of victim cooperation. I figured that'd be the same story as the thefts. But one soliciting charge went to trial. Arturo was acquitted.

From age twenty-two to twenty-five, Arturo had no dealings with the police. Then came the final entry on his record, a felony arrest for fraud. This report popped up in electronic form, courtesy of the new reporting soft-ware that went into place right around that time. I read through it carefully. The Bunco detective was brisk and to the point, detailing a confidence scheme that went sideways and turned into a blackmail scheme instead. The victim was an art collector named Donovan Sloan. Once again, Arturo played the role of secret male lover, working Sloan into a position to be photographed *in flagrante delicto.*

The detective couldn't be sure if Arturo had co-conspirators or if he hatched the plan all by himself. For his part, Arturo dummied up and lawyered up. Sloan initially pressed charges but ultimately requested that everything be dropped. I didn't have to read much between the lines of the detective's report to see he didn't appreciate the back pedal.

So what did we have on Arturo? Four years removed from a con, seven years removed from hustling johns. Now dating a wealthy socialite do-gooder. What was his angle?

It wasn't lost upon me that Sloan was an art collector. Was that what got Arturo going on this latest pose as an artist? Or was that part legit?

I guess we'd find out.

On a hunch, I checked to see who Arturo's lawyer was in the fraud case. I didn't expect to see Martin Shannon's name, but you never know. My suspicions were founded a few moments later when my request came back. Arturo's lawyer name was a public defender whose name I recognized from other cases.

Oh, well. In detective work, you check everything, just in case.

I printed off the short form of his jacket and made a note to ask Coltrane to push through access to his sealed juvey record. I was pretty sure it was going to be more theft or more hustling or both, but we needed to tie up loose ends. Then I ran up his last known address through the department of licensing.

My phone rang. "Moccia," I answered.

"Hello, Detective."

I recognized Bernie Collier's irritating voice. "Well if it isn't the department's least favorite IT tech. I hope you're planning to titillate me with an important development."

"Now who's using hundred-dollar words," he nagged.

"Titillate?"

"Yeah."

"It's got the word 'tit' in it—therefore, it's a thou-sand-dollar word."

"Child."

"Okay, Bernster, what've you got?"

"I requested a subpoena to access the victim's financial records, but it hasn't come through yet. I figured it might explain all the lottery tickets."

"I like your thought process, Boy Blunder. What else?"

"Not much in the browsing history, cache, journal entries, or registries, but someone was online seconds before the Word document was opened."

"And?"

"The user was on glosbe-dot-com, looking for a translation. The final page was a translation and definition of the word *canicula*."

"Which means?"

"It's Latin for 'bitch.' The doer obviously thought about using the Latin word but for some reason changed his mind."

"I don't get why, but it is interesting. Not sure why they waffled?"

"Or vacillated."

"Or equivocated."

"You're getting good at this, Mocha."

"Thanks. You got anything else?"

"No."

"Fabulous. Goodbye, jerkoff."

As I hung up the phone, Winslow returned to his desk with a single sheet of paper in his hands.

"Hey, partner, you about ready to go?" I held up Arturo's address and rap sheet. "I got the scoop on Arturo, and we definitely need to talk to him. I also heard something semi-interesting from Collier."

Winslow thrust the sheet at me. "Save it. He's not the only one we need to talk to."

I looked at the paper. The heading was a Department of Corrections banner. A mug shot stared out at me from just below that. I glanced at the name: "Travis, Leonard P."

"This is Lenny, huh?" I gave him a quick

appraisal. "He looks about like you'd expect a scumbag psychologist pederast to look like."

Winslow shook his head. "Look at the bottom."

I scanned down the page to the final line. The date on it was five weeks ago. The status next to that read "Released."

I looked up at Winslow. "Holy shit. He's out."

"Holy shit is right," Winslow said. "And I think he needs a visit at least as bad as artist boy. Don't you?"

Chapter Fifteen

It took us about forty-five minutes for Winslow to deposit his processed hamburger meat in the precinct john, to saddle up, and get over to the Sheepshead Bay area of Brooklyn. I spotted Arturo Calderas strutting down Emmons Avenue as if he were Joe Cool, the Transitions lenses in his trendy Ray-Bans changing from clear to dark brown as he emerged from the shadows of the OTB betting parlor into the light of day. Did I say strut? Correct that—his gait was more of a swagger, like a man who wholeheartedly believed that he was a stone-cold god, an otherworldly entity so cool that shit would slide off his blazer as if it were coated with Teflon.

As he got closer I realized that I was wearing the same Ray-Bans. I ripped mine off and stuffed them into my jacket pocket so that I'd be able to intimidate Mr. Fancy Pants with my dead eyes, face-of-death expression while I questioned him. The old Italians called it *faccia de morte*, and I had that old school look down cold. I inherited it from my old man who used to make me shit my pants for coming home with a bad report card. Between Winslow and me, we looked like two of the four horsemen of the apocalypse as we walked down the street. Winslow was War and I was Death. We certainly looked menacing enough to terrify an artistic fop like Calderas.

I elbowed Winslow and pointed out our man. "No good cop, bad cop routine on this one, buddy," I said sizing up our mark. "It's Detective Motherfucker and Detective Worse Motherfucker from the get-go. Come on strong. I think this twerp will fold like dollar store wrapping paper."

Winslow nodded. I could see his face turn to stone, which was a beautiful thing to watch. It was as if he had just looked Medusa dead in the eye and made her pee herself.

"Arturo Calderas?"

Our shadows swept over him like a deadly shroud. We already knew that he'd been to the your-ass-is-busted rodeo plenty of times and I could see that he knew exactly what was going down. We flashed our shields. No diehard perp wants to see a pair of gold shields in the bright light of day. It's like holding a pair of crosses in front of a vampire, but as I said, he'd been around the block more than once and played it cool. "Yes. Who's asking?" he asked cautiously.

"Detectives Winslow and Moccia, NYPD homicide. Got time to answer some questions?"

"About what?"

"We're investigating the murder of Jessica Shannon," Winslow explained, deadpan. "You're a person of interest."

Translation: You look good for the murder.

I watched our man's face with interest, hoping that a telltale bead of sweat would break out on his upper lip or forehead.

He seemed slightly shaken. "Jessica's dead?" Was his emotion an act or the real thing? Only an acting coach could tell for sure. "What happened to her?"

"We'll get to that," Winslow said in his hard-as-nails voice. "When was the last time you saw Ms. Shannon?"

"I guess we're getting right into it."

"Looks like it. So how about an answer?"

"Out here?" He looked around, his eyes darting from storefront to storefront before finally settling on a coffee shop. "My friend manages the café. We can talk quietly inside."

"After you," Winslow said in the callous demeanor of a Nazi Gestapo officer. I was surprised he didn't throw in *mach schnell* for effect.

The coffee shop was just a few car-lengths away. From behind, Calderas' strut didn't look so much like a swagger any more. Instead, it looked more like he was prancing.

The coffee shop was no Starbucks. It smacked of independent ownership. Eclectic might be a better word. The floors were painted concrete, the walls were covered with flyer-clad corkboards, and the menu was hand written on a chalkboard. Calderas gave the barista the high sign, who nodded with a look of concern as we marched eyes-forward to the rear of the store and sat down around an Ikea-like table. You have to hand it to that company. Who but the Swedes could build a multi-national conglomerate out of nothing more than sawdust and glue?

Caldera had his cell phone in hand and was already checking messages before my butt made contact with chair. "Hey!" I shot. "They've got an app for people who check their phones when it's inappropriate to do so. It's called 'Respect!'"

He gave me a mild scowl but swallowed nervously at the same time. "Sorry." He stowed the phone in his pocket. "So how can I help you?"

"By answering our first question. When was the

last time you saw Ms. Shannon?"

"Probably a week or two ago, just by chance. I don't see her anymore."

Morgan already told us that he and Jessica had been dating about six months but I figured it was worth two seconds of my time to see if his information jived. "How long did the two of you date?"

I could see him thinking. It appeared that he was about to answer when a tall blonde in a tunic and black leggings came over to take our order. She had a body like a Victoria's Secret runway model, tall and lithe, so perfect that Darwin would've probably classified her as an entirely new species. "Can I—" she began.

I slapped my shield on the sawdust table. "No thank you," I said with a wink.

"Oh. Okay. Sorry." Startled, she turned to leave but over her shoulder, she looked at me in an unexpected way. It was the same look Sandra gave me when we first met. Was it the cop thing she found intriguing or did she just find me devastatingly handsome? Blood began to flow south of the border and I made a mental note to come back for coffee at a more opportune time.

Turning back to Calderas, I rolled forward. "You were saying?"

"A good six months." His answer matched Morgan's, but it was the way he said, "A good six months." That sounded like, *I got tired of her.*

"What happened? Did she want to take the relationship to the next level?"

"Oh, no, nothing like that. Our relationship was casual. I don't think she was looking for anything more than what we had. Only..." He looked uneasy. "I met someone else."

What a lucky bastard. I had the sense that he didn't have any trouble finding women to warm his bed, and when he couldn't find a woman, well...fill in the blank. "So you broke up with Jessica?"

"Yes. About three weeks ago."

"Why?"

He seemed puzzled. "I don't understand."

"Why'd you leave Jessica? I mean she was hot *and* wealthy. What was it? Did you find someone with more money? Better in bed?"

"That's kind of personal isn't it? And what's with the crack about her money?" His tone crackled with resentment.

"Why didn't you just date them both?" Winslow asked in an attempt to bait him.

"I don't—"

Winslow rolled his eyes. "Oh, cut the shit,

Arturo. We've seen your rap sheet and we know that you're not shy about swinging your dick."

"That was in the past," he insisted.

"And now you're an *artiste*, is that it? You're a fine upstanding member of the community who wouldn't contemplate diddling two women at the same time. *Please*, spare me."

"I—"

"How long were you fucking both of them?" Winslow interrupted, hoping for implied agreement.

Calderas squeezed his eyes shut. "About a month." He opened his eyes and glanced at the ceiling. "But I didn't kill anyone."

"We never said you did." Winslow came at him with the force of a jackhammer. "But now that you've brought it up, you got an alibi? Give it to me quick—where were you on Monday morning, and who can we call to confirm your story?"

"The Aurora gallery in Soho."

Winslow grew more aggressive. "*Who'd* you meet with? *What time?*"

Calderas had the answers on the tip of his tongue. "Claude Salinger, the owner. About ten-thirty I think."

"And before that?"

"Before that nothing. I took the subway into

Manhattan at about nine."

"You slept at home?"

Calderas nodded.

"Prove it!" Winslow said obstinately.

"How?"

"Were you home alone? Can anyone verify that you spent the night at home?"

"Just my pillow," he replied, indignity somewhat apparent in his quip.

"Watch the mouth," Winslow said heatedly. "You're pissing me off."

Winslow had come on a little too strong. He had bullied Calderas into a corner and you can only push a person so far before they panic. I knew what Calderas was going to say before the words came out of his mouth. "I don't have to talk to you, not when you're being belligerent."

My eyes flashed at Winslow indicating for him to back off, then turned to Calderas. "Calm down. The more we cover now, the faster we can rule you out as a suspect. We just need a few more minutes."

He took a moment to reconsider. "Okay, but I need a minute." He rose from his chair. "Okay if I wash my face?"

I nodded. Calderas rose and walked toward the bathroom. I turned back to Winslow. "What do you think?"

"I think you want to fuck the waitress."

I smiled and looked over my shoulder to where the tall blonde was drying mugs. She met my gaze and flashed a demure smile. I beamed back, then turned to Winslow and peaked my eyebrows. "No doubt about that one, but what about Calderas?"

"I think he's a slimy womanizing cocksucker, but that doesn't mean he killed anyone."

"He could've prepared himself in advance, but he answered your alibi questions without an instant of hesitation. A quick call to this Salinger guy will confirm his appointment at the art gallery, but he certainly had time to do it before taking the BMT into the city. He inferred that he left for the appointment from home, which means he either took the B or Q train. All the subway stations have security cameras. I'll ask him where he caught the subway from and we can pull the footage for the Monday morning rush hour."

"You inspire me, Mocha."

"Thanks, but as much as I'd like to smack this creep around on general principles, I don't know if he's a killer."

"Maybe, but he still had opportunity. His alibi is far from being ironclad."

I sighed, "That's true."

"By the way, how was I?"

"You were a beast, but while it's a blast watching you go at Calderas like a freight train, I think you'd better dial it back a notch. You've got him pinned into a corner and he's becoming defensive."

"You were the one who told me to come on like a motherfucker."

"Yeah, but not like a worse motherfucker. That was my job." I smiled to let him know it was all right. "Listen, I'm glad you're embracing the role with such zeal but your performance is a little over the top, Pacino."

"Okay. When he comes out I'll ask him if he'd like me to braid his ponytail."

The blonde returned and placed a tray on the table with three mugs of coffee. "On the house," she said as she emptied the tray. She placed a Java Club card in front of Winslow and me. "After seven purchases the next cup is on us." I flipped it over and saw that she had written "Allison, Wednesday through Sunday, 10:00 to 4:00" and her phone number. The seven required purchase slots were already chopped out with a coffee cup-shaped punch.

"Thank you, Allison," I said appreciatively. "You've just made a new customer."

"You don't even know if you'll like the coffee yet," she teased.

"*Oh*, I'll like it. You can count on it."

Her eyes sparkled as she said, "I just made a fresh pot." She picked up her tray. "Enjoy!"

Winslow had a better view of her walking off than I did. "Look at that sweet young ass," he said, basking in the moment. "Can you imagine hitting *that*?"

"Easy, world class dad and husband of the year. You're stepping out of character."

"Jesus, Mocha, I'm only human. Did you see that rear end? It's like it swivels on ball bearings or something. Say, how'd you know her name?" He picked up his coffee mug before noticing that my card was completely punched. "Hey, what the..."

I flipped the card around so that he could see her note.

"Why you lucky son of a bitch."

I took a sip before commenting, "Hey, how long does it take to wash your face anyway?"

"You worried that—"

I was already on my feet. It was a small store and I wasn't surprised to see that there was just one unisex bathroom. I tried the doorknob. It didn't turn but the door moved a hair. "It's dead-bolted, Winslow." I knocked twice. "Mr. Calderas, are you all right?"

Silence.

I rapped on the door again. "Mr. Calderas, I need you to come out of there right now." Turning to Winslow I shook my head. I hesitated for a moment thinking about the damaged property report I was going to have to fill out, then put my shoulder into the door. The cheap pine molding fractured like a week-old cookie. Fresh air hit us in the face. The bathroom window was wide open and Calderas was gone.

Chapter Sixteen

"When I get my hands on that little prick—" Winslow didn't finish the sentence, but he tightened his hands around an invisible throat in front of him and clenched them into fists. He let out a wet, snapping sound.

"Easy, big fella."

"Easy, my ass. He punked us, Mocha."

"He gave us the slip," I allowed. "But punked? That's a strong word for it, don't ya think? At least in the circles we travel."

He glanced over at me. "Y'know, if you hadn't been trying to get laid, maybe—"

"Whoa! I was just sitting there."

"Sitting there trying to get laid."

"I was sitting there with you."

"Trying to get—"

"Sitting there with you," I interrupted, "while you scoped out the barista's ass."

He hesitated. "Yeah, well, she had a sweet ass."

"She did."

The Last Collar

"Heart-shaped," he added.

"I know."

"I always wanted a girl with a heart-shaped ass."

"You're a fucking romantic."

We were scoping out the neighborhood, trying to pick up Arturo again. After spotting the gaping open window, we ran out to the sidewalk to start the search. Of course, I first picked up the card Allison left, and dropped a bill on the table. I could see the excitement in her eyes as I hustled past her to get to the street.

Winslow and I split in opposite directions, went down the street, and turned toward the alley. I thought about walking the alley, but figured anyone as pretentious as Arturo wouldn't be willing to hide among garbage pails. Winslow had no such compunction. He started down the alley from his end, making his way toward me, checking behind cans and dumpsters.

I signaled to him that I'd meet him when he reached my end of the alley, then bolted over to the next street to see if I could catch sight of Arturo in the crowd, but the guy was gone. When I'd trotted back to meet Winslow, his frown told me the same story.

"Drive it?"

"Worth a shot," I said, though I knew it probably wasn't.

So we drove the neighborhood until we were both sure he'd gone to ground for the long haul, or made it outside of the area we were searching. Either way, the little bastard was in the wind.

"Why'd he run?" I asked, more to myself than Winslow.

"Because he's guilty. That's why they all run. Duh."

I grunted.

"What?" Winslow asked from the passenger seat.

"Huh?"

"What was that? That grunt?"

"Nothing."

"Bullshit, Mocha. I know your grunts. You don't agree. So spill it."

"No, I agree. I mean, they all run because they're guilty of *something*, right? But not always what we think they're guilty of."

He ground on that one for a minute or so before conceding. "Okay, sure. They do some dirt we don't know about, we come to talk to them about some other thing that they've got nothing to do with, but they think it's gonna be about the dirt they're actually into, so they rabbit on us. So what?"

"So I just wonder if Arturo bolted because he murdered Jessica, or because he did something else."

"He did it."

"How do you figure that?"

"For one, he didn't bolt right away. And two, all we talked to him about was the murder. Nothing else. He didn't bolt until *after* he knew what we were interested in. That's what had him worried."

"Maybe."

"You got a better reason?"

"Nope. But I'm not ready to charge and book yet, either."

"Suit yourself. I get my paws on him, he's going in the box."

"The box, yeah. But booking?" I shrugged. "We'll see."

"Well, I say—"

"I'm lead detective, so what you say doesn't mean jack shit, huh?" It came out more sharply than I'd intended.

Winslow stopped cold. He sat frozen in the passenger seat, staring at me. Then he said, "What. The. *Fuck*?"

I didn't answer right away.

"Seriously, Mocha, you got a problem we need to work out or something?"

"No."

"Then what?"

"You're giving me a headache."

It wasn't him, though. I knew that. Still, the familiar, painful pulsing behind my right eye had returned. It had started while I was still on the street looking for Arturo and had grown as we drove around in the car. With the pain came easy irritation.

"Well, la-dee-dah, princess," Winslow muttered, shaking his head. "Asshole."

We drove in silence. My head pounded and Winslow pouted. After a while, I realized the pouting was worse than the pain.

"I'm sorry," I said.

"Go fuck yourself."

"No, really. I'm just pissed we lost the guy, is all."

Winslow turned to face me. "Well, maybe you shouldn't chase tail so much, Mocha. It might help you actually do your job once in a while."

I didn't answer. If I did, it could go one of two ways, either playful bantering with an edge, or right back into a real pissing contest. I wasn't up to the latter, so I just said, "But did you see that ass?"

"Yeah," he said, forgiving me. "Heart-shaped."

Chapter Seventeen

We spent the next couple of hours hitting a few of Arturo's last knowns but they were all either out of date or no one there knew where he was.

"Where'd that rat hide?" Winslow grumbled, but he knew as well as I did that there were a thousand places he could be.

"Probably checked into a hotel somewhere," I offered.

Winslow grunted.

"But he has to come home eventually. Or at least come out eventually. Unless he wants to leave his whole life behind."

Winslow cast me a side-long glance. "If he did her, he might run."

"He *did* run."

"I mean really run. Leave town."

I thought about that. Then I shrugged. "A guy like him, the world doesn't exist outside New York. He won't leave."

"You're pretty sure of that."

"Pretty sure."

"So what now? 'Cause I don't feel like going to tell Coltrane that our prime suspect is in the wind. I especially don't want to tell him how it happened."

"Lenny," I said.

Winslow looked at me. "Lenny? Yeah?"

"Lenny," I repeated.

Leonard P. Travis lived in a fringe neighborhood on the border of a middle-class and a lower-class neighborhood. Which direction it eventually went was up in the air, but from the people bustling along the sidewalk, my money was on the upward trend. Which was just what a reformed ex-con deserved, right?

I knocked on the apartment door. Three loud, authoritative raps. The hallway was clean and smelled of wood and some kind of cleaner. The super must be a clean freak.

"Smells nice," Winslow said quietly.

"I was just thinking that."

The light from the peephole blinked. I lifted my badge to it. "Police detectives, Mr. Travis. Open up."

There was a moment's hesitation, then I heard

the deadbolt turn and the rattle of a safety chain. The door swung open.

Lenny was both what I expected and not at all what I expected. Just as I'd seen in his mug shot, he had the face of an intellectual, all round and placid, complete with John Lennon specs. He harbored the beginnings of a sensitive ponytail. But he stood just shy of six feet and instead of the willowy frame of an academic, his build was stocky and well-muscled. He didn't wear a tight T-shirt like most juicers, but his ripped physique was impossible to hide even beneath the long sleeve collared shirt he wore open at the neck.

"Is this about Jessica?" he asked. His voice was calm but a little froggy. I noticed a slight puffiness around his eyes.

"Can we come in?" I asked.

He considered, then opened the door further, and motioned us inside. We walked into a small living room while he closed the door behind us. Winslow casually took out his notepad.

"I didn't kill her," Lenny said, staring at each of us in turn.

"I didn't say you did," I replied. "You mind if we sit down?"

He considered again, but this time he shook his head. "Yes, I think I do mind. I know you have business to accomplish here, so proceed."

"Hey," Winslow snapped. "You want, we can do this down at the station."

Lenny's eyes narrowed. "With my lawyer?"

I held up my hands. "Whoa, Mr. Travis. It's not like that."

He turned to me. "All due respect, Detective, don't bullshit me."

"I'm not. We just need to talk to you as part of our investigation. I'm sorry we got off on the wrong foot there. My partner—"

"Is probably an idiot," Lenny finished.

Winslow bristled next to me, but shocked me by keeping his mouth shut.

Lenny ignored him. "I assume you're the lead investigator?"

"I am."

"Then here's the situation. I know you have to interview me, or attempt to. I also know that given the fact that I was married to Jessica at one time, I have to be considered at least a tangential suspect. So don't give me the wolf in sheep's clothing routine, Detective."

"I'm not."

"But you were about to." Lenny looked at me intensely. "Look, I have a Ph.D. in Psychology from Columbia. I also served seventeen months in

Woodbourne for a sexual offense. But, of course, you already know all of that, don't you?"

"I do. What's your point?"

"My point is that I am an intelligent, educated man who is also well-versed in the criminal justice system from the perspective of an offender. Basically, I am your worst fucking nightmare."

I didn't answer. This was something new. A guy with a real Ph.D. and a street Ph.D. in being a criminal, too. I'd never seen that before.

But I wasn't going to let Lenny know it. "Hey," I said, "you think you're something special? Fine. You think you know why we're here and what we gotta do? Fine. But how about we sit down like adults and have this conversation? Then I can maybe cross you off my list of suspects and move on."

Lenny made no move to sit. "Ask your questions."

I had to admire the guy a little. Letting us sit or not had become a pawn in our power struggle for who was going to run this conversation, and he wasn't backing down. No problem, because we were already in his house, which was a win for us.

"You're right about Jessica," I began. "She was murdered yesterday."

Lenny didn't reply.

The Last Collar

"How did you know about it?" I asked.

"Word travels fast."

"So it does. How did it travel to you?"

He shrugged. "What does it matter?"

"It matters to me."

He sighed. "You don't think this is in the news?"

I glanced at Winslow. I wasn't aware of a news release or anything from the department.

Lenny caught my look. "It's the twenty-first century, gentlemen. Nothing is secret any more, thanks to the Internet. At least not for very long."

"Fine," I allowed. "Describe your relationship with Jessica."

"Mutual disgust and longing."

I blinked. "Uh...what?"

"I believe I spoke English."

"Can you clarify?" I asked, gritting my teeth. This guy was an arrogant wiseass.

Lenny gave me a look usually reserved for the mentally retarded, then explained slowly, "We had a strong mutual sexual attraction. Much of our relation-ship was predicated on that. When we probed deeper into each other's personalities outside of the bedroom, the result was mutual disgust."

I cleared my throat, recalling how Winslow and

I had appraised Jessica's form while at the crime scene. "Okay. Well, the sexual part I don't need any further explanation about. But why the disgust?"

"She disgusted me because she was a phony. I disgusted her because I saw through her and she knew it."

"How was she a phony?"

He gave me a pitiful look. "Detective, please—in the most banal fashion possible, and in the most basic sense of the word. Image was everything for her. Perfection. I tired of it rather quickly, despite her sexual prowess."

"When was that?"

"When was what?"

"When did you get tired of her?"

He sighed. "Much too late to avoid marrying her."

"But you stayed married."

"Officially, yes."

"Why?"

"Initially, because I didn't mind access to her money," Lenny said. "And neither of us really pushed the issue. Then I had larger issues to deal with."

"You mean prison."

"Yes."

"Did you two argue much when you were together?"

"Hardly ever. It didn't fit with her image."

"But occasionally?"

"No. Rarely."

"Any physical violence between the two of you?"

"No. I'm afraid I didn't learn much about physical violence until I was sent to Woodbourne."

I could almost hear Winslow thinking, *Good. Hope it hurt.* Or maybe that was me.

"When was the last time you saw Jessica?" I asked.

Lenny took a deep breath and let it out, thinking. "Well, I saw her from across the room at a restaurant about a week before I was arrested, but we didn't speak. I'm not even sure she saw me. Before that, it had been several months."

"So you haven't seen Jessica Shannon in almost two years?"

"That is correct."

"Any other contact?"

"Not in person."

"Then how?"

"She wrote me letters while I was in prison."

I glanced at Winslow who was scribbling furiously. "What kind of letters?" I asked Lenny.

"Phony ones," he replied. "Vintage Jessica."

"Phony how?"

"Superficial. She wrote as if I were away on an extended vacation to Europe or something, instead of prison."

"Did she want to resume your marriage when you were released?"

"I'm sure she would have, if I'd allowed it."

"You weren't interested?"

"No. The price was too high."

"The price?"

"Yes. Pretending she wasn't a complete charlatan. Living the lie. It wasn't worth it."

"You haven't seen her since your release?"

"As I've already stated, no."

"So you don't care about her anymore?"

"I didn't say that," Lenny said. "I *am* sorry she was killed. It made me sad. I'm still sad. But I don't think I need to share how I feel with the very men who might be trying to affix the blame for her death on me."

"All right, let's cut to the obvious question, then. Can you account for your whereabouts from four a.m. to noon yesterday?"

"From eight until four, I had clients. Before that—"

"Wait. Clients?"

He stared at me as if I were stupid. "Yes. Individuals who pay for my services. They're called clients."

"So you're practicing again? You got your license back?"

"No."

"Then how are you—"

"I am not providing psychological treatment, Detective. I am merely providing informal counseling services."

"Black market therapy?" I gaped at him, a little surprised.

"Hardly."

"This can't be legal."

"It is perfectly legal. And none of your business, I might add, other than to confirm my whereabouts from eight until four."

I shook my head in disbelief at the notion of someone trusting a guy like this after what he did. "Fine. How about four to eight?"

"I was asleep until six. Between six and seven-thirty, I ate breakfast and did yoga. From seven-thirty to eight, I reviewed my notes for my first client of the day."

"I'll need your client list."

"I will provide you contact information for

everyone I saw until noon. After that, it is, once again, none of your business."

I smiled tightly. "You might be a smart guy, Lenny—"

"It's Leonard."

I raised an eyebrow. "Really? The Shannons all say Lenny."

His face tightened into a small scowl. "When I was with Jessica, my life was different. Going by Lenny instead of Leonard...it *softened* some of those differences."

"Made you more a man of the people."

"Precisely."

"Helped you bond with Martin Shannon, did it?"

"*Puh-lease*. Bond with that old prick? I'd rather go back to Woodbourne. No. I tolerated his holier-than-thou attitude because I had no choice. He was a necessary evil."

"Needed his blessing?" Winslow asked.

"Not me, but Jessica...what can I say? Martin Shannon calls all the shots in that family. Jessica lived for her father's recognition."

"But now you're Leonard."

"Yes."

"Because now you have exactly the opposite problem."

"It isn't a problem," he said. "It's a consideration."

"Well, Lenny, consider this. You may be a smart motherfucker, but you're not the motherfucker in charge of this investigation. So you will give me the names of everyone who can vouch for your whereabouts all day yesterday, and if you don't, I will get in touch with your parole officer and let him know what's going on here."

"It's perfectly legitimate. There's nothing he can do about it."

"Maybe, maybe not. But what he can do is climb up your ass and take up residency there. He can check up on you daily, even hourly. And if he finds one small violation, he can revoke you."

Lenny's scowl had grown. "I abide by my conditions of release."

I shook my head. "No one is perfect. You'll make a mistake. Hell, I'll bet you're restricted from having any contact with juvenile females who aren't a blood relative, aren't you?"

He didn't answer. Instead, he stared at me, his eyes hard.

"I'll take that as a yes. Pretty hard to avoid that one, huh? My guess, a vigilant P.O. would find a violation like that within a week, maybe even seventy-two hours. And while the Ph.D. part of you probably doesn't like the injustice of that one bit, the convict part of you knows it true. Am I right?"

Lenny stared cold daggers at me, wordless.

"I'll take that as another yes," I said. Then I took a step deeper into the small living room and sat down heavily on his leather sofa. "I'll just wait here while you get those names."

Chapter Eighteen

"These are some severely fucked up people," Winslow moaned as he checked the third name off Lenny's list. We'd gone straight back to the house after interviewing Lenny and had begun the tedious task of checking his alibi. "There's nothing more tiring than playing cat and mouse with rejects who don't want to admit they're in therapy."

"How many left?"

"Just two. I tried them already and left messages."

"Hand me the list. I'll make the follow up calls. You mind warming up the food?"

"Yeah, sure." Winslow's devoted wife had snagged the results of her husband's latest blood work up in which the big man's cholesterol had risen to two-seventy despite a daily ration of statins. She prepared a high protein, low carb meal for the two of us and dropped it off at the house while we were out conducting inter-views.

"Your missus is as good as gold."

"I know."

"She deserves better."

"I know," he said with irritation.

"Hey, I'm not judging. We all have our failings."

"You're judging. You're always judging."

"Well maybe, but I do it in a nice way."

"Fuck you," he mouthed. "And I mean it in the nicest way."

"Jesus. What's the problem? You *manstruating*?"

"That's adorable. *Manstruating*? You ought to get a job with Fuck & Wagnalls."

"That's Funk. Funk & Wagnalls, shit for brains. I think all that cholesterol is gumming up your gray matter. Maybe you oughta go for a cleansing. You know, where they force feed you lemon water and irrigate your hind parts."

"You know that line, Mocha, the one you've just crossed? Don't be surprised if I spit in your lunch," he grumbled. "And I know it's Funk & Wagnalls. I'm not a goddamn moron."

I flashed my palms. "Touchy, huh? All right. I'll back off. Really though, you okay? What's eating you?"

"What's eating me? We're nowhere on this case. I keep glancing over at Coltrane's office waiting for him to pounce on us."

"Can't stand the heat, huh?"

He pointed to the calendar hanging on the wall behind him. He had penciled in his time remaining and was crossing off the days as they passed. First thing every morning he'd pull out a sharpie and cross off the current days before doing anything else. "Seven months, Mocha—you think you can keep your shit together until the fall? That's all I ask, a quiet ride to the finish line. Can you do that for me?" He started away without waiting for answer.

We were sixty percent sure that Lenny hadn't murdered his ex-wife. Two more calls and we'd be ninety percent convinced. Of course he could've lied about the time he arose, ate breakfast, and the yoga crap, but that would be difficult to check on and my gut told me that although he was an infuriating twerp, he wasn't a murderer. I dialed the next number on the list he'd provided us, the patients he'd seen the morning Jessica Shannon was murdered. Vonda Jones had been his first patient. She picked up after a couple of rings.

"Ms. Jones, this is—"

Click.

"Why you..." I dialed again. She answered and disconnected before I could utter a word. "Ya wanna play like that, huh? That's okay, I've got all night." I dialed again.

"What the hell do you want?" she blurted this time.

"Detective Moccia, Ms. Jones. *Don't* hang up."

"Another cop called and woke me up. What's the problem? I work nights."

"Sorry we disturbed you, Ms. Jones. We simply need to confirm that you visited Leonard Travis at his home office at eight a.m. Monday morning."

"How you know that?"

"We're simply verifying his Monday patient schedule, Ms. Jones. No need to be alarmed. It's purely routine."

"What's routine about being harassed by the police?"

Motherfucker. "A simple yes or no will do, Ms. Jones. Were you there or not?"

"Don't I got patient confidentiality?"

"This has nothing to do with you and we have no interest in your reason for visiting Mr. Travis. As I said, we simply need to confirm that you were there at that time. We're verifying his whereabouts."

"Why? What's he done?"

"Nothing. It's simply routine."

"Now you've got me nervous. Should I stop

seeing him?"

"No. I mean, not because of this phone call. Like I said, it's strictly routine."

"I know he's been to jail. He was up front about that, but I never asked what he did. Should I be afraid? Did he rape someone?"

Oh dear Christ. "You'll have to have that conversation with him, ma'am. Now for the last time, did you see him or not?"

"I can look that up online, right?"

For the love of God, would you please just answer the damn question? "I'm going to hang up now, ma'am, but before I do could you *please* just say yes or no?"

"*No.*"

"*No* you weren't there?"

"*No* I won't answer until I know what this is all about."

"Have a good day, ma'am, and thanks for your cooperation." It wasn't until I hung up that I realized Winslow had returned with our dinner.

"Couldn't help notice your use of excessive sarcasm. What's going on, you can't conduct a simple phone interview without sending the caller into apoplexy?"

"Apoplexy is speechlessness caused by extreme anger. Vonda Jones was not angry and she certainly wasn't speechless. She's nuts, a lithium tab short of delusional."

"I'm sure she was one hundred percent normal before she got on the phone with you."

"I'm sure she was one hundred percent normal blah, blah, blah." I shook my head trying to rid the exasperating Vonda Jones from my mind. "Fucking job." Redirecting my gaze toward the Styrofoam dish of food Winslow had placed in front of me. "What the hell is this?"

"A lentil-barley burger and a salad. It's all vegan."

"Seriously," I groused. "Isn't vegan synonymous with dog shit?"

"*Hey!* My wife made this, asswipe. At least try it before you complain."

"You're right, you're right. Got any ketchup in your drawer?"

"It's seasoned. How do you know you need ketchup?"

"Because I put ketchup on everything. Gee, defensive much?"

Winslow looked in his drawer and flipped me a package of Heinz. "There. Happy?"

"That's all you have?"

"He shook his head, searched in his drawer, and threw another at me. "Enjoy, dickhead."

"You wouldn't happen to have a bun in there, would you?"

"No. No bun."

"It's not a burger without a bun. It's sacrilege." After covering the burger with copious mounds of tomatoey goodness, I cautiously tried a bite. "Hey, that's not bad."

"Thank you, *moron*."

"What's for dessert?"

"I don't get dessert until I get home later. I have to space out my meals."

"Shit. Just because Sarah wants you to live to be a hundred doesn't mean that I have to live a monk's lifestyle. I wonder if they filled the vending machine with Twinkies. I hear they're back in business."

Winslow was three molars deep into his vegan burger patty when the color drained from his face. No explanation needed—I knew that Coltrane was standing behind me before hearing him speak. His sinister aura preceded his deep, rumbly voice. It was like being in the presence of evil—Coltrane had come to suck the life from us.

"What kind of shit are the two of you eating?" he asked with a confrontational wrinkle of his nose. "Smells like that kimchi crap Sergeant Park is always eating. You two turning into biscuit heads on me?"

"Ten-four, Lieutenant. I've got an appointment to get my sidewalls shaved this evening. I figure the Kim Jong-Un thing is popular with K-girls at the local rub and tug."

"No seriously," he came back. "Smells like the gas from the horse Kramer fed Beef-A-Reeno."

"Uh, Lieutenant...Winslow's wife prepared it. It's a healthy alternative to hamburger."

"I see." I figured Coltrane was going to offer up some manner of meager apology but he didn't. He went straight for Winslow's jugular. "You know a couple laps around the gym would do the same thing and you wouldn't be straddled with eating buckwheat."

I snorted.

Fuck. Why did I do that? He's going to figure it out and—

"What's so funny, shit for brains? Did I say something funny?" He shut his eyes when the revelation hit home. "Why, you childish motherfucker."

Winslow flipped me the bird. "Yeah. Fuck you, Mocha."

I started to laugh. Then I choked on the veggie burger and tears ran down my cheeks. "Couldn't help it. I just pictured you with Buckwheat's junk in your mouth."

"All right, all right," rumbled Coltrane. "Let's get serious, jerkoffs. Where do we stand on the Shannon file?"

"We interviewed her ex, this afternoon. He's a dick-wad pedophile but he probably didn't kill anyone. We're just about finished verifying his alibi."

"What else?" he asked impatiently.

I shrugged.

"You're kidding? That's all you have for me."

I shrugged. "What can I tell you? This vegan diet has me feeling a bit lethargic." I could see that Winslow was having a cow. I really didn't care what Coltrane had to say but I didn't want to get Winslow's considerable ass in a sling. "We're going to try to rundown Calderas after we eat. We figure we stand a better chance of finding him at night." I had just told the lou an out and out lie, a complete fabrication, but the man was a beast and I figured I'd throw Calderas at him as a sacrifice. Most perps are dumb enough to think they're safe on the streets at night, because it's easier to hide in the dark. So that's when they come out to play.

"Do I have to remind you that Mr. Shannon has executive command's ear? Do I have to remind you that they're on my ass? What do I have to do to motivate a couple of lame dicks like you?"

"We're on it, boss. We're covering all the ground two detectives can cover. Of course, we wouldn't complain if you put together a task force..."

"Task force my ass, Mocha. I told you I'd give you all the support you needed and what have you asked for? Nothing. I want a list on my desk first thing in the morning. Whatever you need to close the case." He began to saunter off. "And eat that dog shit somewhere else," he barked. "Bad enough I have to put up with your bad breath day after day, Mocha."

Winslow waited until Coltrane and his menacing aura had vacated our space. "That was ballsy of you."

"Ah, fuck him. He can take his holier than thou rhetoric and shove it up his overdeveloped ass."

"Jesus, John, what's gotten into you? That's his standard rap. I actually think he let us off easy."

"That's because I placated his ass with the Calderas story."

"I was going to ask you about that. Nice impromptu line of horseshit. Hey, what's with the puss?"

"I shouldn't have shot my mouth off. You're seven months from the finish line and I'm putting your ass in jeopardy. Sorry, bud, that was selfish."

Winslow shrugged, as if to say, *So what else is new?*

Chapter Nineteen

We bounced around the same tired ideas for another half hour while I choked down the disgusting imitation burger drenched in ketchup. I kept any further wise-cracks to myself, for a couple of reasons. One, I could tell that Winslow was reaching his threshold for my shit and any more would put him over the top. I just wanted to razz the guy; I didn't want to hurt him. Secondly, I was starting to feel like hell. Not another headache, though the threat of one lingered just offstage, but an overwhelming sense of guilt blanketed me, guilt for risking Winslow's future, which really translated into risking his family's future. I also felt guilt for my own family situation. Which was, in a word, fucked. I even felt a little bit guilty for not being further along in this case. If I didn't know better I'd say my hormones were out of whack.

That last guilt was the one I didn't want to shed. Someone died—in this case, Jessica Shannon—and no one was going to speak for her if Winslow and

I didn't. It's a strange and sacred trust that's placed on the homicide detective. The victim doesn't choose who to place that trust with. Hell, most victims probably couldn't imagine they'd end up murdered. But in some posthumous way, by default, the victims have no choice but to trust a guy like Winslow or me to represent justice for them.

And how do we respond? With tired resignation—just another stiff, another DeeBee in a long line of them. Or so we try to tell each other and ourselves so that we can keep our sanity. But that's bullshit, because every murder I've ever investigated sticks with me. Every one of them has driven me to try to find out who the killer is. Early on, that drive was such that I could show everyone how badass I was, how wicked smart a detective I was, how none of these other motherfuckers were fit to carry my jock. And there was still some of that, if I'm honest about it, but the bigger piece now was about finding some justice for that victim. And if I wasn't successful, and it made me feel guilty? Well, then, *good*. That's the kind of angst that keeps me sharp.

The guilt that goes along with Winslow, or my family, though...I didn't feel like carrying that load around, and I had an idea how to help me forget about it.

By the time Winslow and I had repeated ourselves at least twice on every angle of the case we could come up with, I made a show of turning my wrist and looking at my watch.

"It's getting late, partner," I said. "Let's catch some shuteye and hit this hard tomorrow."

"You really want Coltrane seeing us bail out of here without any progress?"

"We made progress. We discussed the case. We've got a plan."

"I guess I missed that part," Winslow said. "What's the plan?"

"The plan is to come back fresh tomorrow and hit it hard. Didn't you just hear me?"

Winslow shrugged. "Fine. I'm beat, and Sarah will be glad to see me home for a change. She figured we'd be pulling a double."

"Hell, we're already over our regular shift. We're not going to solve this one falling asleep at our desks."

Winslow rose, brushing remnants of his meal off his shift. "See you tomorrow, then."

I waited until he'd started to walk away, then called out his name. He glanced back at me wearily.

"Tell her thanks for the veggie burger," I told

him.

He gave me something between a snort and a laugh, then left.

I immediately reached for the phone.

She answered on the third ring, and we made a plan in less than ninety seconds. The plan didn't matter, though. It was just a premise to get me to knock on her apartment door. I think we both knew we weren't going out to listen to any jazz or see some play or whatever it was she'd suggested on the phone.

By the time I got to her apartment, the headache that had been threatening off stage all day finally raised the curtain and started its performance. Sometimes when I get them, the pain comes in a throbbing rhythm, which is horrible but manageable. I just do everything in between the beats—talk, listen, chew...breathe. But this was one of the other kind, the constant humming pain that slowly rises in intensity until I'm nauseous. Sleep is about the only thing that puts a dent in one of those beauties.

Thankfully, as I knocked on her apartment door, the hum was still low and weak. I heard the soft pad of foot-steps and saw the peephole wink to darkness and then light again. A moment later, the deadbolt rattled and Allison swung open the door.

She was still wearing the same clothes as at the café earlier in the day, and they still fit her better than the manufacturer intended. She flashed me a smile. "Hey, you!"

I gave her my best John-Moccia-is-the-man-of-your-dreams grin in return. "Allison," I said, drawing out her name like I was some New York version of Matthew McConaughey. "Great to see you."

She waved me in. Her apartment was tiny but clean, and it was decorated in that way that single women have with their living space with tons of knick-knacks and decorations but without seeming cluttered. I wasn't sure how they did it. I couldn't put two magazines on my coffee table without the place looking junky.

"I'm not quite ready," she said. "Can I get you a beer while you wait?"

"Sure."

She went to the fridge and made a show of leaning forward to pull a bottle off the bottom rack. My gaze traveled up her calves and legs to her beautiful ass. Her beautiful, heart-shaped ass, as Winslow had taken great pains to point out. I felt a dark throb of lust at the thought of getting my hands on it. A small ping of pain in my temple answered, almost as if in counterpoint.

"Light beer okay?" she asked without turning around. Her hips rocked slightly while she searched the fridge. "I don't seem to have anything else on hand."

"It's fine. I prefer light."

She turned around, a bottle of Heineken Light in her hands. I immediately noticed that the cold from the fridge had done its work. Her nipples protruded from the thin T-shirt like bullets.

"I figured you might," she said. "Gotta stay in shape to chase the bad guys out there, right?"

I smiled. "That's right."

She handed me the beer. "Well, it shows."

Jesus, this was going to be easy. I could have probably leaned in for a kiss right then, but the small, jagged pinging in my temples stopped me. I decided a little beer first might be the solution. I raised the bottle. "Got an opener?"

"Oh." She actually blushed. "Duh."

She reached into a drawer, fished out an opener and handed it to me. I nodded my thanks and popped the top. The crisp coldness felt good at the back of my throat, and I welcomed that first small flush of warmth in my stomach.

Allison held out her hand.

I thought about it, then put the bottle opener and cap into her palm. She didn't miss a beat, replacing the opener and tossing the cap into a garbage can under the sink.

"I just need a few minutes," she said, smiling again.

"No problem." I wondered if she thought I was actually so obtuse that I'd missed her signals. I raised the beer. "I'll wait."

She left the small kitchen area and went through a bedroom door a few strides away. I noticed she swung the door closed behind her but not all the way. It stood ajar, cracked open a few inches.

I moved into the living room and sat on the edge of a loveseat. An onyx kitten played with a ball of string on the coffee table. The figurine was either stylish or childish. I couldn't decide which.

"Have you ever seen Miguelito play?" she asked from the bedroom. I could hear her opening and closing drawers.

"No," I called back.

"But you've heard his music, right?"

"I don't think so."

"Really? He's huge right now, at least here in the city."

"And where else is there?" I mused, half to

myself.

"What's that?"

"Sounds great," I said, louder.

"I know, right?"

Through the crack in the door, I saw her pull the shirt over her head, revealing the thin red strap of a bra across her back. She threaded her arms into a black sweater before pulling it over her head, then moved out of view.

This would be the time I was supposed to ask her something about her job. How long had she worked there? Or maybe the suave approach of asking in genuine tones what was it like to own a coffee shop these days. She'd laugh at my assumption and confess that she didn't own the place but was only a waitress. Or if she had high self-esteem, she might say she was a barista instead. I'd apologize and explain that I figured a woman so put together as her would be the owner. That might be enough. Hell, with this one, it almost certainly would be. But maybe she'd need another jest or two. When it gets to the tipping point, some women pull back momentarily, as if to convince someone in the room that they're not actually that easy. Whether it was me she wanted to convince or herself, I couldn't say, but either way I don't think anyone was fooled.

And who cares, anyway? I didn't understand this game. Oh, I knew the rules, and I could play it like a pro. But why? As in the *big* why? Why do we have to play it? To satisfy some outdated social more about the chastity of women or some such nonsense? I mean, if I wanted her and she wanted me, why couldn't we just be honest about it? We both knew the score. The game was just a façade.

And yet we played.

It made my head hurt some more just thinking about it.

She came out a few moments later, her high heels clacking on the floor. Winslow once said the height of a woman's heels was directly proportional to her desire to get fucked that night. That qualified as advanced math for my partner, but I couldn't argue with the equation. And by the look of Allison's shoes, solving for x wasn't going to be a problem.

"Sorry to keep you waiting," she said, flashing that dazzler of a smile again.

"Some things are worth waiting for," I said, cringing inwardly as soon as the words left my mouth. But I punctuated it with a smile of my own.

She turned her head slightly to the side. "Aw, that's sweet."

Sweet? It was maple syrup on double chocolate

cake. It was enough to give me diabetes just for saying it. "I'm just a sweet guy, I guess." I took a final sip of my beer. I figured we were leaving now or we weren't but either way, the beer had served its purpose and was finished.

She took a seat beside me. "Not many of those left in the world. Sweet guys, I mean."

I set the bottle down and shrugged. "We set the bar kinda high for membership."

She touched my arm, gave it a little shove. "You're silly."

"Sweet and silly. The two esses."

She affected a seductive expression. "Make it three. Sexy, too."

I leaned in and kissed her softly on the lips. The first one was confident but hesitant, nothing invasive, a statement and a question at once. I felt my temple throbbing in time with my heartbeat, which had quickened, but only slightly.

When I pulled back, our eyes met and I waited. The next move was hers. That was the rule, the steps that this dance took. She knew it and I knew it, and so we held that smoldering gaze for several long seconds before she came in again for the return kiss.

And finally, *finally,* we could abandon pretense for a little while.

We'd started on the couch but ended up in her bedroom. Afterward, I lay back on one of her pillows, catching my breath and trying to enjoy the afterglow in spite of my headache. She curled up next to me, her head finding my chest.

You can tell a lot about a woman by these moments. Or at least, you can tell what she's looking for. The ones who curl up like Allison did are looking to latch on. The fucking was all fine and good, but there was more to it than that. She was hoping to turn this great first encounter into a mythical "how we met" marriage story.

Yeah, I'm a shit when it comes to women. I knew it, too. Hell, Sandy was proof enough of that. But if it wasn't, there was a long line of pinch hitters to help seal my status as exactly the raging asshole she had me pegged for.

Case in point. I was lying in bed with a beautiful woman who had just scored a nine-point-three in sexual gymnastics, actually making me feel good for the first time in a week. A woman with a heart-shaped ass, no less.

And me? I was wondering how long I had to lie there before I could leave. Worse, if I was still going to have to attend the goddamn Miguelito concert. The pounding in my head had gone from a light throbbing ping to more of a hammering like a blacksmith on an anvil. The last thing I needed was to sit and listen to some music I had never heard of played by some schmuck who was pretentious enough to have only one name.

Allison stirred on my chest, and I knew what was coming, an offer of a shower and a suggestion that we could still make the show. Or did I want to go dancing? Like I needed the thump of a bass right now. Or maybe she was about to talk about how she never did this, or how special it was.

Jesus, the whole thing made me nauseous.

That's when I realized that it wasn't just figurative. I could feel the nausea rising in my chest, swirling in time with the increased pounding in my head. All the good after-sex feeling washed away and I winced. My free hand went to my forehead.

Allison glanced up at me. "Are you okay?"

I started to shake my head, but bells went off when I did. Giant, clanging church bells.

Allison's expression went from sleepy seductress to panicked inside of a second. "Omigod! You're white as a sheet. What's wrong?"

I sat up slowly and swung my feet over onto the floor. I needed some cold water. Maybe on a washcloth. Allison could get me some ice. That would be even better. Ice at the base of my neck would help. It would—

That's when the nausea struck again, a brutal counterpoint to the blasting throbbing in my head. I slid forward, landing on my knees. The explosion in my head sent shock waves through my body. Before I realized it, my stomach clenched and I vomited. Beer and the remainder of Sarah Winslow's veggie burger splatted onto the floor and against Allison's night stand.

"Omigod!" She yelled in disgust. "What's wrong with you?"

I couldn't answer. I wouldn't have told her what it was even if I could have formed a sentence. I was sorry for the mess, even as I knelt there on her floor, the blinding pain in my head almost causing me to faint and the second round of vomiting moments away. I was sorry, but the reality is that vomit cleans up. It goes away. Even the smell would be gone soon. She'd go on with her life with nothing more than a weird memory about the cop that she fucked so hard he puked on her bedroom floor.

That brought on another retch. Almost nothing came up this time, just a few small chunks and viscous liquid. But the all-over body clenching had the same effect on my head as the first one. I reached out blindly for support and caught a hand on her nightstand.

"Fuck!" Allison shrieked. "Go into the bathroom, asshole! Use the toilet!"

I drew in a ragged breath. Large white dots fluttered and danced in my vision.

Maybe this was it. Maybe this was finally it.

"What's wrong with you?" she repeated.

Everything, I wanted to say. Instead, I took another labored breath through my torn throat. Then I forced myself to say one word.

"Ambulance," I croaked.

Then I fell forward, vaguely aware of landing face first in the warm puddle of my own vomit before I passed out.

Chapter Twenty

I'd been to the ER plenty of times in my career. As a patrol cop, I took innumerable reports from victims who were robbed, assaulted, or even raped. Becoming a detective didn't change that very much, as I still saw the inside of the emergency ward frequently. Catch people early on and interview them before they have time to concoct a story, that's was my motto. Didn't matter if it was a victim, witness, or suspect. It was a sound approach no matter how you cut it.

I was no stranger to the ER as a patient, either. Unless you decide to be a precinct rat, never venturing out into the field, chances are the bad guys are going to get a lick or two in on you over the course of a career. I was better at that part than some, worse than others, which meant I had to be patched up a few times due to on-the-job injuries. Those injuries usually ended up being a source of professional pride, like a scar on a hockey player's chin. Honestly, most of the time the worst part of that experience was doing the Labor and Industries paperwork.

This was different.

I woke up briefly in the ambulance but the sound of the siren put me over the edge again. Or maybe they gave me something. I wasn't sure. But when I finally woke up in the hospital, I was in a narrow, glass-walled room only about twice as wide as the bed I was in. It took a moment for me to recognize it as the ER. The view was a little different from that perspective.

"Good morning."

I turned slowly toward the clinical voice, half expecting my head to explode, but I felt nothing.

No, that wasn't quite true. I felt a pressure. Maybe an ache. But I also felt a little spacy.

Ah, Christ. They had me on dope.

The voice belonged to Dr. Hal Stiviak. He sat in the chair to my right, legs crossed, and without his doctor's smock.

I licked my lips and swallowed dryly. Then I rasped, "Hey, Doc. Buy you a drink?"

"No, thanks. But let me buy you one." He leaned forward, picked up a plastic cup full of water and held it out to me. I took it, surprised at how weak my arms were, and sipped from the straw. The water felt glorious.

Dr. Stiviak leaned back and waited. I took a couple more sips from the straw, then lowered the cup to my lap, still clutching it in my hand.

"They call you out?" I asked.

He nodded. "As soon as they pulled up your records in the computer."

"I figured."

"Do you want to tell me what happened? Your girlfriend wasn't much help at the scene."

"Not my girlfriend," I said.

"That might explain why she didn't ride in the ambulance. Or come down to the hospital."

Strangely, I felt a slight pang of sadness in my chest over that.

Jeez, I *was* an asshole.

"Did it come on suddenly?" Dr. Stiviak asked me.

"Yes."

"Preceded by physical exertion?"

I tried to manage a sly smile but I'm pretty sure what I ended up with was more of a grimace. "You could say that."

"Recent stress?"

"Plenty."

He nodded slowly. Then he drew a deep breath. "John, I think it is time we move to the next level in your treatment."

"Treatment?" This time the grimace I gave him was the perfect expression for what I wanted to communicate. "That's what you call bombarding my brain with radiation?"

"It's a valid method to reduce the tumor size."

I drew a wavering breath and let it out. "Yeah, remind me the odds of that?"

He didn't reply.

"And while you're at it, even if you can shrink it, the odds that I'd survive brain surgery to remove the goddamn thing?"

He didn't drop his eyes. I'll give him credit for that. He stared at me calmly and said, "They're low."

"Five percent to reduce the tumor, that's what I remember you saying."

"Five to fifteen," he corrected softly.

"And even if that horse comes in, my odds after going under the knife were what? Three percent?"

He hesitated briefly, then nodded.

"So basically, there's better odds that the Yankees are going to relocate to Mexico City than me successfully surviving treatment."

He stared at me expressionless for a moment. Finally, he said, "No matter what the odds are, John, they are better than the odds you have of surviving without any further action. Those odds are at zero percent, and you know it."

"I've survived this long."

"You have," he agreed.

"And you don't know how long that will last."

"You're right. Not without a crystal ball."

"So we're right back to where we were at my last checkup. I'll take the unknown odds on living an indeterminable time period over the odds on a surgery that are to the right of the decimal point."

"That's your prerogative. But as things progress, you can expect more episodes like the one that occurred this evening. Our best strategy is to apply the first stage of treatment. At best, it may improve our options. At worst, it will improve your quality of life."

I raised my eyebrows and was surprised when that didn't hurt. Must be good dope they were pumping into me. "Quality of life? Somewhere I think I heard that chemo doesn't exactly enhance quality of life. Unless you're the kind of guy who likes being weak, hairless, and puking all the time."

"It's up to you, John."

"Glad to hear it."

"But there's something else to consider."

"What kind of flowers I want at the memorial service? Because I'm thinking hydrangeas."

"No. Your job," Dr. Stiviak said.

A wash of cold water splashed down my spine.

No.

Don't take that from me.

I swallowed. "So I guess we need an exit strategy there, huh?"

"Exit strategy?" He shook his head. "No, John. It's time to notify the department and put in your medical retirement paperwork. You've reached a point where it isn't safe."

"My job is never safe," I said, resigned.

"It's not safe for other people any more, either."

I was quiet for a long moment. Then I said, "Not to be a dick or anything, Doc, but don't I have some kind of patient confidentiality? I mean, I could swear that every time I need medical information for a case, some doctor tries to shove HIPAA up my ass."

Dr. Stiviak nodded. "There are confidentialities, yes, and you have the right to limit how much detail I share with the department."

"I'd prefer none."

He shook his head. "I can't do that."

"I don't get it. You're not the department doctor. You're *my* doctor."

"And that is one of the two reasons why I must make a notification."

I held up hands and dropped them in frustration. "That makes no fucking sense."

"John, you're my patient. I have to do what is best for you. You are experiencing symptoms that could be highly dangerous if they manifested themselves during a critical situation."

"Like what?"

"A physical encounter with a suspect, for one. But even driving a vehicle is problematic at this point."

I thought about it, but realized I couldn't argue with him. I could lie about the symptoms and their severity, which I'd done, but now that he was up to speed, his logic was undeniable.

"Fine, I get that. But what's the other reason?"

"My oath isn't just based upon one patient. If I am faced with a situation that places other people in danger because of my patient, I'm obligated to take preventative action."

"That sounds like bullshit."

"Think of it this way. If you had an infectious disease, what would be my responsibility to the public? To quarantine you, notify everyone you'd come into contact with, and give a general warning through the Bureau of Public Health."

"Brain cancer is catching now? Because it's not like I have Ebola."

"No," he said patiently. "But you're in a high risk profession. And your medical status places people in danger."

I blinked at him, thinking. The guy was difficult to argue with.

"I'm sorry, John. But I have to recommend you be relieved of duty pending medical retirement. I probably should have done this a month ago, but your symptoms weren't manifesting themselves, and..." he trailed off.

I thought about all the headaches and nausea episodes over the past several months that I hadn't told him about. How lucky I'd been to keep them at bay while I was on the job. What a decent guy Doc Stiviak was, and how I'd put him in a tough position.

Still, that didn't stop my next move.

"You're right, Doc. It's time. But I need to do this my way, okay?"

He looked perplexed. "Your way? John, there's only one way to—"

"No, there's not." It came out sharper than I intended, but Dr. Stiviak didn't react. I guess when you spend a lot of your time around dying people you grow some thick skin. "Look, if you just send paperwork over there, it'll be a big thing, right? Everyone will hear about it, but not from me. And worst of all, it'll be *them* telling *me* the way things are going to be. That's not how I want to end things."

He hesitated, then shrugged. "All right, but I still don't see—"

"Give me the paperwork," I said. "Let me take it to work with me. I'll go to my boss and get assigned to desk duty. That takes care of the issue of what's safe or not, doesn't it?"

He didn't reply immediately, so I forged ahead.

"Once I'm on a desk, then I'll get everything in order, and turn in your paperwork along with my medical retirement packet. *I'll* tell *them* how it's going to be. That's how I'll end things with the job."

He considered, watching me. I gave him the most earnest expression I could muster. Finally, he said, "How long will that take?"

I shrugged. "Maybe a week, at most."

He considered some more.

I waited.

"John," he began. "We've talked about the stages a person goes through when confronted with a scenario like this. Denial comes in many forms. So does bar-gaining."

"Jesus, Doc. I'm not in denial, and who the fuck am I going to bargain with? The Tumor Depot?" I put my thumb and pinky to the side of my face, miming a phone. "Hey, guys, I changed my mind. This tumor's not working out. Come and get your shit out of my brain."

He didn't reply.

I sighed and dropped my hand. "It's not what you think. I know the stages. I'm at acceptance. Have been for a few months. Reluctant acceptance, sure. Pissed off, even. With a big dose of procrastination, too. But the reason I want to handle things the way I do at work isn't about that. It's that there's...there's people I want to talk to before everyone gets wind of this."

This time he nodded in understanding. "And you need a week to accomplish this?"

"This and the paperwork piece, yeah."

"One week." It wasn't a question.

"At most."

"On a desk."

"Of course."

"All right," he said. "One week, and then if I don't hear something from the department, I'm faxing over my recommendation."

"No problem," I assured him. "I'll have it taken care of by then. I promise."

He accepted me at my word.

Doctors. For all their God complex, and all that

they experience, most are still hopelessly naïve about human nature.

"Who have you already told?" he asked.

I smiled. "No one. That's the problem."

Dr. Stiviak took a deep breath and let it out. "Well, then, Detective. You have some work to do."

I kept smiling.

He didn't know the half of it.

Chapter Twenty-One

"Anyone coming to pick you up?" Stiviak asked rhetorically. More than rhetorically – cynically. He listened to my heart and took my blood pressure one last time before studying the release papers and scribbling his signature.

I glanced over his shoulder while buttoning the cuffs on my shirt. "Nice signature, Doc. I see you've completed an advanced course in hieroglyphics."

"Yes. It was a course prerequisite at Cornell along with symbology, semiology, and progressive avarice for the career-minded health professional."

His signature may have been pure chicken scratch, but avarice...not a chance. The doc was one of the good guys, one of those rare individuals who took the Hippocratic Oath seriously, a real mensch.

"You do know that handling the department is one thing, but it wouldn't be a bad idea for you to tell some-one about what's going on with you. You must know at least one person you can entrust with your secret."

"*Why?*" I asked obstinately.

"Because it'll come as a tremendous shock to your loved ones if you there's an unforeseen tragedy."

I raised a leery eyebrow. "Loved ones?"

"Cut the shit, John. Your parents are still alive and I know for fact that you've got a little girl."

"A little girl who hardly knows me."

"Maybe this is a good time to set things right. I mean there are plenty of cops out there who can pick up your case files." He stared into my eyes. "John, wouldn't your time be better spent getting reacquainted with your daughter?"

"So it is time to put my affairs in order."

"I told you, my crystal ball is out of commission. But..." He filled his lungs and exhaled noticeably. "We have to be realistic about this. You've got a very serious condition."

"You give this kind of advice to all of your patients?"

"Only the ones that require it." He smiled sadly. "Whether we're talking about next week or the next century, when the time comes you need to leave the world knowing you tied up all the loose strings in your life, and your work...well that's just your work. Don't even think of leaving this world estranged from your daughter."

"Jesus, Doc, that's one dump truck full of guilt you just dropped on me."

He approached and laid a hand on my shoulder. "Get your priorities straight, John. There aren't any do-overs once you've passed on to the other side." He smiled sadly, then turned and left the room.

God gave me a great day—bright sun, singing birds, and every other wonderful fucking thing nature had to offer, everything I'd soon be saying goodbye to. I glanced up at the big guy. "Thanks, you son of a bitch!" Man that stung—pretty girls with heart shaped butts, blue skies, and sunsets...all swirling and on the way down the drain. I could almost hear a giant flushing noise in the background.

I'd already gotten three calls from Winslow. I hadn't answered any of them and there was no need to listen to the messages to know why he was calling. I sent him a text saying that I had an emergency and that I'd get in touch with him in a couple of hours. Despite all the weight Coltrane had laid on us I knew Winslow might still crawl up my ass for a couple of hours of personal time, and if he did…

No. I wouldn't do that. I wouldn't whip out the death card. It was too soon.

Stiviak had done a most effective job at fucking with my head. Instead of thinking about Jessica Shannon's taut little corpse growing colder and colder in the cadaver fridge, I was thinking about my little girl and my folks, the only living breathing humans besides my partner that I gave a shit about. Maybe that was the right thing to be thinking about. Shit, of course it was the right thing to be thinking about. I was in denial about the entire mess and too arrogant to accept the cards I'd been dealt. I couldn't imagine Winslow's reaction when he found out that I'd be banging out before him. Geez, how lucky can a guy get?

I could've hailed a cab but I didn't. I decided that if my days were numbered I'd better milk all the happiness and beauty out of each one that I could. My folks lived less than a mile from the hospital, and with a fresh regimen of drugs coursing through my bloodstream I figured that I was stout enough to walk. I stopped at the Italian deli and picked up all the items I knew they liked, especially the ones that were expensive, the one's they normally passed up buying unless it was a special occasion.

Jesus, what do I tell them? What don't I tell them? I tried to come up with something reasonable to say, just enough to brace them in case I took a sudden dirt nap, but not enough to send them over the edge. My dad's cousin lost his son in a boating accident and my folks often spoke about how hard it must be to lose a child. I didn't envy my folks or the days ahead—the poor God-loving bastards, they were about to find out the hard way.

Chapter Twenty-Two

My father's mouth dropped and his cheekbones rose when he saw me standing at the door. He unlatched the jalousie door, pushed it open, and threw his arms around me. "Giovanni!" he shouted robustly and kissed me on my cheek like the old school Italians do. "Carolyn," he boomed. "Our boy's here."

"Ah," she shrieked from the kitchen. "Johnny? I'm coming. I'm coming."

Dad was exactly my height and just a tad narrower, not skinnier, just more compact. He was coming up on his sixty-fifth birthday and would've been considered to be in fantastic shape for a man twenty years younger. He attributed his vitality to clean living, peace of mind, a glass of red wine with dinner, and the fucking turtleneck sweater.

I was in a shirt, tie, and blazer. Yes, the stuff I'd worn on my date with Allison. My clothes, along with hers, had been abandoned on and around the living room couch and as such had avoided an Earl

Scheib vomitus paint job. I presumed that I had been taken to the hospital *au naturel* and it was pretty obvious that Allison had taken a pass on the ambulance ride, so how my personal items showed up at the hospital was beyond me—not that I'm complaining. Dad glanced unhappily at the shirt collar and tie, no doubt worried that I had tempted fate because I had abandoned my turtleneck.

Mom was drying her hands on a dishtowel as she hurried toward me. "What a wonderful surprise. What happened, Brooklyn run out of bad guys?"

"Fat chance," I cracked in a cynical voice, wrapped her up in my arms, and planted a juicy one on her cheek. Mom was petite in stature, only about five-two—her height had always bothered her. Other than bedroom slippers she didn't own a single pair of flats. She wore two-inch heels at all times and considered five foot-four a legitimate height for a woman. She was up on her toes and still only up to my chest.

She peeked into the grocery bag. "What did you bring us?" she asked eagerly. Rather than offering an item-by-item inventory I handed her the bag and let her poke around on her own. "Italian bread, imported prosciutto, provolone, olives..." She dug further down into the bag seeming giddy with joy. "Fresh mozzarella, stuffed artichokes..." She looked up into my eyes. "What's going on here, Johnny? Is everything all right?"

"Of course everything is all right. I was in the neighborhood. I figured we'd have an early lunch before I went back on the clock."

She seemed skeptical. "You're sure?"

"Of course I'm sure. You want to break out the sodium pentothal and a water board? God, but you're a bloodhound."

"Easy does it." She examined my face. "You look pale. And you're too skinny. Are you feeling all right?"

"Why don't you set the table? I'm starving."

She finally backed off but I could see that her sense of concern was clearly unsatisfied. She smiled in spite of it. "I just made a pot of minestrone. This is perfect," she cheered, before turning and walking off.

My dad put his arm on my shoulder and walked me into the house. "The Mets are up by two. You been following the series?"

"No. I've been busy. Who are they playing?"

"'Who are they playing?'" he mimicked disbelievingly. "The Dodgers, knucklehead. You too busy for baseball? Since when?"

"Since we got a second TV," I groused.

"The great American pastime isn't good enough for you anymore?"

"I'd rather watch grass grow."

"*Fannable*," he grumbled. "You used to love baseball."

"I used to love Soupy Sales too but..."

"Okay, okay, don't lump the two of them together. I get the message."

I smiled warmly hoping to lure him into a trance. "Hungry, Pops?"

"Hungry? I'm a Moccia. I was eating *capicola* when I was still in the womb." He opened a kitchen cabinet and reached for a liter jug of Chianti.

I held up a hand. "None for me. I'm going back on the clock in an hour."

"For real?" he asked with a grimace. "You can't handle a little glass of vino?"

"Of course I can," I barked. "It's just..." *With all the new meds coursing through my veins I'm afraid I'll puke my guts and go in to my passing out routine.* "I've got a lot of ground to cover this afternoon. The lieutenant has his head so far up my ass he knows what I had for breakfast."

"Madonna, Giovanni, no wine and no baseball? Your life has turned to shit." He tore the end off the fresh semolina bread, chucked some of it into his mouth, and washed it down with a sip of wine.

Mom had set a table fit for royalty. In five minutes she had plated all the delicacies I had purchased and supplemented it with soup and a wedge salad. "*Mangia*," she exclaimed as she settled into her chair.

We said grace, dove right in, and ate like *gavones*.

My mom took a bite of the sandwich she'd made and placed it back on her plate. "We spoke to Sophia last night, John. She's beginning to sound like a big girl."

I smiled weakly. Despite the fact that Sandra cut my balls off at every opportunity, she'd permitted my parents to remain close with her. Not close as in drop-ping her off for the weekend close but as in reach-out-and-touch-someone close.

"We call twice a week just before going to bed. With the time difference we catch her right after she's had her dinner," she continued.

"We just sent her cookies from the Italian bakery," my father volunteered. "Your mother wraps them in foil and Saran Wrap."

"They stay fresh?"

He nodded.

"Sandra says Sophia loves them," Mom said with a smile. "Have you talked to your daughter recently?" she asked half-scolding.

"It's been too long," I confessed. "I've been wrapped up in this case, and if Sandra picks up we get caught up in our holy war and the phone never makes its way to Sophia."

"That's disgusting," my father swore. "Get on a goddamn plane and go see her, for Christ's sake. She's your daughter, Giovanni. You're going to let a spoiled marriage stand between you and your daughter? That doesn't sound like the son *I* raised."

I sighed and dropped my soupspoon into the bowl. "It's not as easy as it sounds. Sandra turns the simplest things into a holy nightmare."

"Bah!" he grumbled. "I'll talk to her."

"Go ahead, but she'll only cut you out of the equation. Once you take sides you become the enemy. She's three thousand miles away. Remember?" We were at an impasse—they both absorbed my comment and continued to eat while searching for an answer that didn't exist.

I was glad that they both drank wine with their meals because as much as I wanted to keep my mouth shut, I knew I had to tell them something. I procrastinated as long as I could but finally reached the point of no return. They had both finished eating. Mom had a peaceful expression on her face and Dad's hand was stuffed into the waistband of his slacks. I opened my mouth, initiating what I knew would be a true come-to-Jesus moment. "So look. I've been having these headaches and—"

"Oh dear Lord. What's wrong?" she blurted cutting me off. "Is it an aneurism?" Her face turned white. "Your uncle Carmine had an aneurism. My God, is it hereditary?"

I was almost tempted to say yes. I mean after all, it sounded a hell of a lot better than brain cancer. What's a measly little arterial bulge compared to the big C? Nothing right? It's like a pimple on an elephant's ass. Cancer on the other hand is an ever-widening chasm filled with misery.

"*Madonna mia.*" I looked at my father. He looked frightened. "Son, what did they find?"

"They found a mass," I said in an offhanded manner attaching as little importance to the discovery as possible. "They want to do more tests."

They both fell silent and then looked to one another their eyes filling with tears.

"Hey. Who died?" I quipped. "The two of you look like hell."

"What kind of mass, son?" my father asked, his voice low and grave.

I shrugged. "They don't know yet. I guess the doc hasn't made enough payments on his Benz yet. You know how these doctors are, they order tests and refer their asshole buddies. They do a dance with the insurance companies to get their tests authorized. It's one great big circle jerk."

Normally, my mom would chastise me for language like that, but she remained silent, watching while my dad laid his hand on top of mine. "Son," he said quietly, "is this cancer?"

I wanted to lie. I wanted to say it was too soon and that the doctors just didn't know. I wanted to say anything to spare them pain, but in the end, I nodded, and then we all cried.

Chapter Twenty-Three

I've walked out the front door of my parents' house hundreds of times over the years, but it was never harder than it was today. My mother clutched at me, weeping, reaching up, and hooking her hands behind my neck while she pressed into my chest. I held her for long minutes while my father stood behind her, silent. His wounded expression was every bit as difficult for me as mom's crying.

Finally, I peeled myself away from my mother, told them both I loved them, and walked away. I didn't look back. Not once. I just walked up the street and around the corner, where I hailed the first cab I could get.

"Where to?" the driver asked.

I gave him the precinct address. He dropped the car into gear and headed there.

In my pocket, my cell phone was buzzing again.

The Last Collar

At the station, I made my way to the detectives' bullpen. Despite the crushing sadness that had surrounded my confession to my parents, I felt strangely lighter now. It was as if by sharing the news some piece of the burden had been lifted. I guess keeping it to myself had been more taxing than I realized.

As I walked through the door into the bullpen, I put on my game face. I'd already decided I wasn't going to tell Winslow until I absolutely had to, and certainly not until after we settled out the Shannon homicide. If my career was coming to a close, I was going out on a win.

"Mocha! Where the fuck you been?" Winslow sat at his desk, the phone pressed to his ear and the mouthpiece tilted below his chin.

"I was having lunch with my—"

"Hold on." He held up his finger and moved the receiver in front of his mouth. "Yeah? Go ahead." He scratched something into his notebook. "Okay, I got it. Thanks, Smitty."

I waited until he hung up before asking, "What was that?"

Winslow pointed at me. "No, you're not off the hook. Where were you?"

"I told you."

"No, you didn't. You started to."

"I was having lunch with my folks."

He scowled, his eyes narrowing slightly. "In the middle of a case, you just decide to take some lost time?"

"Use it or lose it, right?"

"But we're supposed to be—"

"Look," I interrupted. "You've got a wife and family to go to. I've got my parents. They don't stay up late anymore, so if I want to see them, it's gotta be lunch. And...I needed to see them."

"Everything all right?"

"They're both healthy. It'd just been a while." I pointed at the list on his notepad. "Now, whattaya got?"

He waved at the pad dismissively. "Most of it is crap. Davis called back with the financial audit. It was a big zero. Jessica Shannon wasn't filthy rich, but thanks to her parents, she was comfortable."

"Obviously."

"Yeah," he said absently, checking off an item. "Nothing suspicious going on with her finances. And I ran down some witnesses regarding her charity work. Struck out there, too."

"Oh-for-two."

His expression changed to one of satisfaction. "But I did get a line on Arturo. He's hiding out at some independent gallery over in the meat packing district."

I brightened. "Really? How'd we get that?"

"Some chick named Camille called it in. That was Detective Smith from the Three-Seven on the phone. He took the message, checked the want sheet, saw we were looking for the little shit, and he called over."

"Stroke of luck," I muttered.

"Luck is ninety-seven percent of what solves cases."

"Sweat and shoe leather is what solves cases."

Winslow stood up and put on his jacket. "Don't you know anything, Mocha? Sweat and shoe leather is where luck comes from."

A Tout le Monde was located up a narrow flight of stairs between what used to be two butcher shops back in the day. One was now a music store and coffee shop while the other was an art gallery.

Gentrification. Someday Weird Al Yankovic ought to do a song to the tune of Carly Simon's "Anticipation." Not that most people would get it, but I think it'd be funnier than shit.

The door at the top of the stairs was closed but not locked. Winslow and I let ourselves in. The small entry way was barren except for a minimalist desk to one side. Long, burgundy drapery hung across the opening deeper into the establishment.

A woman with short hair and frameless glasses watched us, unimpressed. She'd been writing something on a notepad, and held her pen poised to continue. "May I help you?"

I flashed my badge.

She didn't react. Instead, she looked down at the desk in front of her, flipped to a clean sheet of paper, and resumed writing. "In my world, sir, that means exactly nothing. Do you have an appointment?

Winslow stepped forward. "In your world?" he rumbled. "Missy, you're in *my* world now."

"My name is Camille," she said primly, her tone otherwise unchanged. "Not Missy. And I'm sorry, sir, but Dani only shows work by appointment, except for scheduled shows. And those are by invitation only. He's very strict about it."

"We're not here to look at what some jerkoff scribbled with a crayon," Winslow told her. "We're here—"

"Do you have a search warrant, sir?" She set down her pen and tore off the sheet of paper.

Winslow hesitated. "No," he admitted. "But I don't need one."

"Perhaps I should telephone Dani's attorney?"

The Last Collar

She held out the paper toward me.

It took me a second to follow what was happening, but when I got what Camille was up to, I cleared my throat and grabbed the piece of paper from her. "That won't be necessary," I said, motioning for Winslow to keep talking. For once, he was quicker on the uptake than I was.

"You know, I can be back here in an hour with a warrant," he said.

"You must be very efficient," she told him.

I read the note.

He's hiding in the closet next to the bathroom. Destroy this.

"I could do you for obstructing an investigation," Winslow said.

"Tubby, you couldn't do me in a fantasy," she replied.

Winslow turned red. "You little—"

"We just need to talk to...Dani, was it? Is he back there?" I folded the paper over and slid it into my pocket.

"As I said," she began, then motioned at the drapery with her head, "he's not to be disturbed."

"Fuck this," Winslow said.

He stepped forward and snapped the drapery aside. A short hallway opened up into a large open room. Art or something pretending to be, hung on the walls and on pedestals throughout the open area.

"Hey! You can't go in there!" The woman stood up in protest, playing her part to the hilt. "Dani!"

I stabbed my finger at her. "Sit down or go to jail," I growled.

She gave me a stunned look that was pretty convincing. Without another word, she sunk back into her chair.

Winslow and I made our way through the large showing area. I could tell by the architecture that there was a room in each corner. As I drew closer, I saw a half-open door leading to an office. A pair of stocking feet was visible through the crack, propped up on the arm of a sofa. I peeked in, and saw a pudgy man in his fifties wearing large headphones. His eyes were closed and his toes were twitching in time with whatever music he was listening to.

Across from the office were two doors. I opened the first and found a small bathroom. The door next to that was a deep closet. Numerous empty hangers dangled from a rod, and some cleaning items were close to the door. I snapped on the overhead light and like a magic trick Arturo appeared in the back corner.

He sighed, his shoulders slumping in defeat.

"Goddamnit. How'd you find me here?"

"We're brilliant detectives," I told him. "Now come out of there."

He worked his way out of the corner and dodged the hangers. I pulled him from the doorway, pushed him against the wall, and snapped the cuffs on him. Then I handed him over to Winslow.

"Hello, fuckface," Winslow said. "Remember me?"

"I remember your breath," Arturo said, but his comeback didn't have any zip to it.

"Yeah, you're a funny guy," Winslow said. "Let's go."

Winslow walked Arturo out, taking every opportunity to jerk him one direction and then the other along the way. I hung back, stopping at the front desk.

"If you're going to continue to harass me—" she started, but I held up my hand to stop her.

"Don't bother, Camille," I said, my voice low. "He's in his office with headphones on."

She didn't reply.

After Winslow was done dragging Arturo down the stairs, I turned to the receptionist. "Why'd you give him up?" I asked.

She frowned. "What do you care?"

I didn't answer, but I kept looking at her.

Finally, she said, "How about this? People shouldn't act like they give a shit about somebody just to get something they want, and then suddenly forget who they are. That work for you?"

"As good as anything," I said. "Thanks, Camille."

At the station, Winslow tossed Arturo in Interview Four while I grabbed a cup of coffee. I rubbed my throat absently, wishing for my turtleneck. Maybe it was seeing my dad and being reminded of how he got me on that kick as a kid, or maybe I was just being Linus with a security blanket but I almost went down to the locker room to see if I had a spare hanging in my locker.

Coltrane changed my mind.

"You two collared up, I hear?" he said, scowling. His gruff voice barked out what most would consider a compliment, but I knew better. And how'd he know about Arturo already?

The answer came in a flash. The desk sergeant must have called up to him when we came through the front doors. Nice to know whose side that weasel was on.

"Not a collar," I told the lieutenant. "We

grabbed up the artist for questioning."

"Second go at him." Again, not a question, but more of an accusation.

"Yeah, well, the first one ended abruptly."

"I know. I read the report. Rookie mistake, Mocha."

Most of the time...hell, almost *all* of the time, I liked my nickname. But when he said it, I hated the thing. I felt like screaming at him, "Call me Detective Moccia, you browbeating bully prick asshole son of a whore!" But I kept it together.

Instead, I said, "The basic mistakes are always the hardest ones to avoid one hundred percent of the time. Besides, the window he crawled out of was barely large enough for a Siamese cat to fit through."

"You know what they call an exaggeration like that, Detective?"

"The truth?"

"No. It's called an external attribution. That's where someone always seems to find something other than himself to blame when things go wrong."

"You taking some online classes, El Tee? That sounds like something right out of chapter three."

Coltrane's scowl deepened. "You want to watch that smart mouth, Detective Moccia. You're not

Teflon."

Now he calls me that. Of course.

"You're right," I agreed. *More than you know.*

Coltrane shifted gears, back to business. "You like him for the Shannon homicide?"

"I haven't ruled him out."

"That's not an answer."

"It's the only one I've got."

"What did I just warn you about? You want me to bench you on this one? Plenty of other homicide dicks who wouldn't mind a swing at a high profile case like this."

I sighed. "Lieutenant, if you replace me now, you'll set the case back at least three days while the new detective gets up to speed. Even if you make Winslow lead, it'll still take him a day and a half to bring the new guy along as a second. It isn't practical."

"Maybe not, but it *is* possible. So answer my goddamn question."

I took a sip of my coffee, watching him over the rim. He seemed about to burst, but not in the normal I'll-pull-your-head-off-because-I-spend-all-my-time-at-the-gym sort of way. There was a nervous vibe to the man, which was distinctly foreign.

He was feeling the heat from above. That was

the only explanation.

In that moment, I almost felt sorry for the ball buster.

Almost.

Still, I didn't need him up my ass. So…

"Lieutenant, it's like this. We're weak on suspects in this one. The artist looks good because he dated her, because he's been on the con in the past, and because he bolted from us during our first interview. We're going to go at him and see what we can turn up. There's smoke there, but I don't know if there's fire."

Coltrane considered what I'd said, then leaned in close to me. I could smell the strong peppermint on his breath and the clean odor of his soap. "If there's no fire, you better fucking light one, Mocha. You get me?"

I blinked. Was he asking me to…?

No way.

"Find the fire," he said with finality, then turned abruptly and stalked away.

I was still standing there holding my coffee cup when Winslow walked up to me.

"What's up, partner?"

I shook my head slowly, staring after Coltrane. "I just had the weirdest conversation with Coltrane, ever."

Winslow scrunched his eyebrows. "What happened?"

"I don't know exactly," I said, every word deliberate. Then I looked over at Winslow. "But let's go crack this nut."

Arturo seemed less nervous in the interview room than he had been at the coffee house. That told me a lot about his character. He opened his mouth as soon as we walked in, but I held my hand and stopped him. "Hold your tongue, young sir. You're going to want to hear what we have to say before you decide what words should come out of that mouth of yours."

Arturo gave me a strange look, then glanced over at Winslow.

Winslow shrugged. "He's a weird cat. You should try working with him."

Arturo turned his gaze to me and leaned back in his seat. With his hands, he made a flourishing gesture. "Go ahead," he murmured.

I sat down across from him. Winslow moved to the other side of the small room and leaned on the wall just behind Arturo. He positioned himself enough to the side so he'd get caught in Arturo's peripheral vision at times. It was a classic set up to both keep the suspect focused on the interviewer but still off balance, and it almost always worked.

"I'm curious, Arturo. What's your real preference? Boys or girls?"

He smirked. "Neither. I'm only attracted to adults."

"Ah. Well, then, men or women?"

"Why? You looking for some ass?"

I smiled. "I am looking for someone's ass, but not in the way you mean it. See, the reason I'm asking is that I'm curious how it goes for you. When you're scamming some old closet queen out of his cash, do you just grit your teeth and endure it? Or is that what happens when you're working some lonely rich girl like Jessica Shannon? Which one's work and which is enjoying your work, if you know what I mean?"

"Can I smoke?" Arturo asked, his tone bored.

"No."

"That's ridiculous."

I shrugged. "Thank the feds for that. Now, are you going to answer my question?"

He leaned forward and stared into my eyes. "Is this professional or do you have some unresolved curiosities brewing under those Italian good looks, Detective?"

"Purely professional."

"Uh-huh." He leaned back. "What does it matter? I am not into all of the repressed bullshit American society foists on us about choosing one or the other. I am attracted to beauty, in all its forms."

"So you'd fuck a nice looking end table?"

He sighed. "Really? Is this a police station or a junior high? I thought you had something important to say to me. If not, maybe I should just call my—"

"Why'd you break up with Jessica Shannon?" I interrupted before he could drop the magic L-word.

He stopped. After a moment, he said, "It wasn't working."

"How so?"

"How do these things usually not work? Or did you marry your fourth grade sweetheart?"

I had, actually. Well, almost, but I wasn't about to tell him that, or about how messed up things were with Sandra now. But I got his point.

"Fair enough, but be more specific."

He shrugged. "Why?"

"Because she's dead, and you're a suspect."

He stopped again, this time for a longer pause. Then he sputtered, "You can't think...I didn't...*Jesus!*"

"What did you think, Einstein? That we were bringing you in here to talk about it because we *didn't* think you did it?"

"I'm a witness," he said. "I can't be a suspect. I didn't kill her."

"A witness, huh? What'd you see?"

"Nothing."

"See, that's a problem. Most witnesses, they saw something."

He took a deep breath. "At first, I thought you were investigating me for...other things, or that you would, if they came to light. It's been my experience that the police will use just about any leverage they can on a mur...on a case like this."

"A murder?"

He pressed his lips together distastefully and swallowed. "Yes."

"How can you be a witness if you didn't see anything?"

"Person of interest, then."

"Oh, you're of interest to us," I assured him. "Believe it."

He shook his head. "I didn't see anything, I don't know anything, and you're wasting your time trying to get something out of me. There's nothing."

"Why did you break up with Jessica?" I

repeated.

"Oh, for Christ's sake." He looked away, then back at me. "She was a monogamist, okay? A straight, monogamous woman, who was not going to accept that I was neither straight nor monogamous. I broke up with her to spare her the emotional trauma of finding out the hard way."

I sat, digesting what he said.

He didn't give me much time before asking, "Can I go now?"

I held up my hand. "Not just yet. So you're saying this was a mercy breakup?"

"That's exactly what I'm saying."

"And who else were you seeing?"

"Does it matter?"

"It could. Maybe one of them was the jealous type and knew about Jessica."

"Really? Then why wait until a month *after* we broke it off to do the deed?"

I didn't have an immediate answer for that. Winslow tried to rescue me by leaning down into Arturo's space. "What, you're a detective now? How about you leave that to us?"

"Because you're doing such a stellar job of it?" He looked back at me. "You're wasting your time with me."

"I get paid by the hour," I said absently. Then I

leaned forward and lowered my voice. "Who was the new person, Arturo? You told us at the café that you were banging both of them for a while. Tell me who."

He looked uncomfortable for the first time since we'd entered the room.

"Who?" I pushed, raising my voice just slightly.

"No," he whispered. "It wasn't someone, okay? It was several someones. You get me?"

"Any of those someones might have a reason to go after Jessica?"

He shook his head. "Not a chance."

I grabbed a notepad from the corner of the table, flipped it open, and pushed it in front of him. Then I pulled a pen from my pocket and slapped it on top of the notepad. "Write 'em down."

He hesitated, then picked up the pen, and scratched hurriedly on the pad. When he was finished, he thrust it toward me.

I looked down at his flowing script.

Go fuck yourself, you guinea asshole.

I looked up at Arturo. "This pains me," I said. "I thought we were making progress."

He stared at me defiantly.

"You know what?" I said. "Let's pretend this ugliness never happened." I tore the page out of the notepad, balled it up, and tossed it to Winslow.

The big man caught it deftly and it disappeared into his fist.

"I want—"

"What you want is for us to stop thinking you're a suspect, Arturo. You want us to start thinking you're the wrong guy and for that to happen, you've got to give us the right guy. See how that works?"

He sighed, leaning back in his chair. "Jesus, I am so tired of dealing with you people."

"Saying 'you people' isn't nice. It has prejudicial overtones."

"Yeah, you would know," he snapped back, but without much bite. Then he took another deep breath and let out another sigh. I was about to tell him to cut the drama when he said, "Look, I don't know who did it. It wasn't me. I shouldn't have given you guys grief and I shouldn't have run from you, but it wasn't because I had anything to do with this."

"Why, then?"

"I'm working, okay? More than just on my art. You get me?"

I thought about it. "The gallery guy? The ones with the headphones?"

"Yeah, the headphones. Dani so loves listening to his Rush."

The Last Collar

"Working how?"

He met my gaze meaningfully. "Same as before. Except instead of money, I'm trying to get my art shown."

"And if that doesn't happen?"

"Then there's still money as a fall back."

I nodded in mock approval. "Nice plan."

He didn't reply.

"No, really." I leaned back. "My, but you are a cold bastard."

"No colder than anyone else in this city."

"Oh, I don't agree. I think you are much further down the spectrum of sociopathic behavior than the majority of New Yorkers."

"You don't get out much, do you?"

"Touché. And when I do, all I meet are scumbags like you and baristas with heart shaped asses."

"Good for you. Now, I've told you everything I know, so—"

"No, you haven't." I pushed the pad back in front of him. "You may be certain your lovers didn't have an axe to grind with Jessica, but I need to be sure."

"I'm sure."

"That's nice, but *I* need to be sure." I pointed to the pad. "Names and contact info. Now."

He paused, thinking about it. Then he took the pad and wrote very deliberately. When he pushed it back toward me, I knew what it would say before I even looked.

The block letters screamed up at me.

LAWYER!

And after that, there wasn't anything left to say.

"He's hiding something, the little prick," Winslow huffed as we sat down at our desks.

"Thank you, Captain Obvious. He's hiding who he was banging while he was seeing Jessica Shannon."

"Maybe. Or maybe that's what he wants us to think."

"What are you saying?"

"I'm saying I don't like this little shitbird."

"Me neither. But do you *like* him?"

Winslow scratched his cheek where stubble was already popping out. "Something's not right with him. I just can't pin it down. But could I like him for this?" He nodded. "Yeah, I think I could."

"There's not enough probable cause to arrest him."

"Who's being obvious now? I know that, Mocha."

"And his lawyer will be here in—" I glanced at my watch. "Twenty minutes, tops. You want to go at him again, hard and fast?"

"I'd love to, but without something new, and his lawyer being on the way? No, that's no good."

"So we kick him."

"To hell with that. Let his lawyer make the trip and spring him. We can tell the desk sergeant on the way out."

"Out where."

"I'm hungry."

"No veggie burger today?"

"I ate it for lunch."

"So now you want a second lunch? What are you, a hobbit?"

He raised an eyebrow. "You really think I'm going to be home for dinner tonight?"

He had a point. "All right, let's slip out of here before Coltrane comes asking for an update."

"Now you're talking."

Chapter Twenty-Four

"The fuck is wrong with you?" Winslow asked.

"Come again?"

"You've got a rack of baby backs staring you in the face getting bone cold. Something wrong with it?"

"I ate a big lunch."

"Yeah. I remember that, lunch with the folks. Still, you usually make quick work of smoked meats."

I didn't have much of an appetite. Shit, I didn't have any appetite. I felt like my bitch of a baby mama had probably felt when she was pregnant—she lost her lunch just looking at food...food being prepared on TV...an oil painting of a bowl of fruit. I felt like I'd ralph if I ate anything else and I didn't want to lose my cookies in front of Winslow. I pushed the ribs in his direction. "Help me out—my eyes were bigger than my stomach."

"Jesus, Johnny M passing up food. This is a first. Someone kick you in the balls or something?"

The Last Collar

"Yeah. Life," I moaned. "Caught me right between the legs."

Winslow reached into my plate with his knife and fork, and hacked of a trio of ribs. He put one in his mouth, in and out, like sucking ice cream off a pop stick. "They are a little dry," he opined. "I think they had the heat up too high."

I sipped some ginger ale. I was so nauseous I could feel it creeping into my bones. *Probably the new meds. I hope. Or is it the tumor growing inside my skull like the arms of an octopus?* "That's what you get when you order the daily special at the Greasy Spoon. Anyway, you think you'll be able to move your bulk out behind the table anytime soon? Coltrane's ready to offer a blood sacrifice and I don't want it to be me."

He said fuck off with his expression and sucked the meat off his second rib.

"God, you're a spectacle. The way you deboned that rib...I bet you could suck the feathers off a chicken if you were hungry enough."

"Eat shit, Mocha. What's with Coltrane now?"

"Just more of the same—the long arm of the brass is reaching up his ass and he's doing the same to us. Tell you the truth he looked pretty rattled. He told me to make something happen."

"In those words?"

"No. In my words. I couldn't tell you in his words because I'm not a big black prick."

"So the ends justify the means? Any means?"

"Pretty much. I say we check out Arturo's story tonight and then we hit Lenny the dipshit again tomorrow morning."

"I guess the El Tee really got to you. All of a sudden you're hot to trot."

"Stop complaining, would ya? You're the one that whines like a puppy every day. You should be happy I'm ready to get with the program."

"You're a strange bird, Mocha." He looked over his shoulder and air scribbled, indicating to the waitress that we wanted the check. "This one's got a fine ass also," he alleged with raised eyebrows.

Despite my weakened state I managed to rise out of my seat high enough to ravage said fair maiden with my eyes. "That's a piece all right."

"Good as Allison's?"

Now why'd he have to mention her name? As if I didn't have enough goddamn guilt on my shoulders, the mention of Allison's name made me envision the poor thing on her knees scrubbing puke out of her bedroom carpet. I certainly screwed the pooch on that one—nice girl and she fucked like a porn star on the first date. *Shit,* I mused. *I'll have to send her a dozen roses and a Bissell Carpet Cleaner...some Airwick, too.*

I reached for my wallet but Winslow waved me off. "I've got it. You can pick up dinner tomorrow."

If there is a tomorrow, I lamented.

Aw, suck it up, shitbird. You ain't dead yet.

Chapter Twenty-Five

I readied my hand to ring the doorbell. "Here goes nothing."

I didn't know if showing up at Allison's place unannounced was a good idea, but I figured I didn't have anything to lose. I mean what was the worst that could happen? I get rebuffed. I wasn't there for a follow up fuckfest. Bringing her a bouquet of flowers and one of those sappy "I'm Sorry" cards was the very least I could do. I mean I couldn't go to my grave without at least apologizing to the girl.

It's a funny thing about the Big C. The doc tells you you've got it and you think, *Shit. This is the end.* But then time passes and you're not feeling much different and you start believing that maybe the doctors were wrong. I mean that's the human condition, isn't it? Ignorance is bliss and all that. You tell yourself, *This ain't so bad. I can beat this.* But you can't and one day, like the evening I spent with Allison, the motherfucker reaches down real deep, tears your guts out through your eyeballs, and suddenly you know this thing is playing for keeps. Never in my wildest dreams did I think I'd ever lose my shit after making love to a beautiful young woman, but I did, and I knew if given the chance the same thing might happen again.

I rang the bell and listened to the sound of her bare feet, her delicate young feet with her turquoise toenails, padding toward the door eager to see who was visiting. A long moment passed after I imagined she had looked through the peephole. "I don't want to come in, Allison. I just wanted to say I'm sorry." An even longer moment passed before she undid the chain and twisted the doorknob.

I half expected her to slam the door in my face but she didn't. She pulled the door open fully and began to mist up when she saw the bouquet of flowers peace offering in my hand. She stepped forward, threw her arms around me, and crushed the bouquet between us.

"Hey," I kidded. "I paid a fortune for these roses."

This is one hell of a fine person, I said to myself. *Maybe this is heaven already: a gorgeous caring woman and unconditional affection. A guy could do worse. If only we had more time, maybe it could even turn into love.*

She took her time before pulling away. "Come on in, John," she said, her eyes tender, her smile soft and vulnerable. I closed the door and followed her to the kitchen where she filled a vase with water and submersed the stems. I noticed that all the windows were open and the curtains were blowing into the apartment. She opened the card. It contained one of those lame, lovesick poems schlock card writers churn through the grinder like pork sausage. Below it I'd written, *I'll bet you thought I was kidding when I promised you a night to remember.*

I had wrestled with the idea of adding LOL to the end of my note but I was as comfortable with web acronyms as a chimp wearing boxer shorts. Maybe I should have as it might've lightened the mood. Instead, my note brought forth a torrent of tears.

"Whoa. What's with the water works?" *Jesus. What did I do? Can't wait to see her reaction when she finds out that I'm dying.*

"I'm so sorry," she said, then snatched a wad of paper towel from the roll, wadded it up, and pressed it to her eyes. "All I can think about was the way I treated you last night." She buried her head on my shoulder. "I was such a jerk."

I put my hand under her chin and lifted it.

"You? You were the jerk? Gee, what was *I* thinking?"

She smiled a bit but still look very sad. "I didn't think you'd call me again. I was so mean to you. You were sick and all I was concerned about was my—"

"Hey, hey. Give it a rest. I ralphed everywhere. For Christ's sake, you're probably still airing the place out."

"I know, but you were sick. I didn't even go with you to the hospital. I'm such a selfish bitch."

This is why you should stay away from nice girls, I told myself. A guy wouldn't have to think twice about leaving a self-centered, whining trollop, but a girl like this...

You stupid ass, you slept with this girl and now she cares for you. What can you offer her other than front row seats at your wake?

"Why don't you go sit down inside." She blotted her fresh tears. "I need to freshen up."

"Sure. Sure. Take your time."

Several minutes passed before Allison came out of the bathroom. She'd changed into a Rangers jersey, which she wore with denim shorts. She had washed her face and had enough confidence to skip putting on makeup. She sat down next to me on the sofa as delicately as a settling feather with her long legs folded under her. "Are you going to tell me what it was?" she asked in her young, sweet-girl manner, and her eyes twinkling with both inquisitiveness and worry. She rubbed the back of my hand. "Was it just a bug, or...?"

She might've just as well had her hand in my pants because I began to stiffen. *Don't do this!* I warned myself. *This girl is sheer goodness and your lifeline has all but run out. Don't make it any worse than it already is.* "It's way too soon in our relationship to start talking about it."

"Hey, I spent three hours in the laundry room. You owe me an answer." She lowered her head and rested it against mine.

So there I was, this tough-as nails-cop, the kind who kicks ass and takes names, and suddenly I couldn't keep my mouth shut. I guess it was because outside of my folks, she was the only person in my life that was being nice to me. "Listen, Allison, what I've got...well it's not good, and it doesn't get better. I'm sorry. I didn't realize it had gotten so bad. If I had I never would've—"

She silenced me, "Shhh." Allison didn't ask another question. She didn't pry and she didn't break down on me as I thought she would have. She just pulled me into her arms and held me, and didn't let go.

Chapter Twenty-Six

I waited for Winslow the next morning, standing outside my favorite coffee shop and sipping some exotic brew that I couldn't pronounce. It tasted good, though. Everything tasted good. Everything felt good. Funny how that works when you're on the way out.

He pulled up in an unmarked that even some rube from Iowa would make as a police car. Not that we were in the stealth business, but I sometimes wondered why we went to the effort when everyone knew our car for what it was the moment they saw it.

I slid into the seat and held out a cup to Winslow. "It's Quixote, or some Aztec word. I don't know."

"Arabica?" He took the cup and eyed me queerly. "What's up with you?"

"Nothing. It's morning. This is coffee."

"Not that. You."

"Me what?"

"You're fucking glowing."

"Glowing? What am I, a blushing bride or some-thing?"

"You tell me, princess."

"Shut up and drink your coffee."

He did as he drove us to Leonard Travis' house/office. When I rapped on the door, I made sure it was loud enough that it would be as unmistakably law enforcement as the car we were driving.

"Police!" Winslow bellowed anyway.

A few moments later, Lenny opened the door. "I'm with a client."

"Reschedule, shitbird," Winslow told him.

"Get a warrant, *shitbird*," Lenny snapped back. His chest bowed forward slightly, and his fists tightened. The cords in his forearms bulged.

Winslow shifted forward.

I held up my hands. "Let's not do this again. We just want to talk, Mr. Travis."

"We did talk," Lenny growled. "I answered your questions."

"Well, now we have some more," Winslow interject-ed. "And if you're so goddamn innocent, you shouldn't have a problem answering them, right?"

Lenny shook his head at him, his expression

dumb-founded. "That's perfectly Sherlockian logic. I'm *so* impressed."

I leaned forward and got his gaze. "Hey," I said. "I know he's no Holmes, but it *does* have a certain logic to it, no?"

"No," Lenny said.

But he stepped aside and let us inside anyway.

The place looked the same as on our previous visit. Lenny kept us waiting while he went into another room and then ushered a fragile looking young woman out the door, promising her a new appointment.

"She looks awfully young, *Doctor*," Winslow observed.

Lenny flashed him an irritated look. "You want to check her ID?"

Winslow waved him off.

After his client left, Lenny let out a long sigh. "Okay, gentlemen. I have another appointment in..." He checked his watch. "Twenty-eight minutes. I won't be cancelling or postponing that one. So what are your questions?"

I took out a pen and my notepad, motioning for Winslow to take lead.

"How well do you know Arturo?" he asked.

Lenny shook his head, his expression registering no recognition. "Sorry, who?"

"He dated Jessica."

"And I would know him how?"

"I thought you two maybe went to the same gym."

I had to grin a little at that, but Lenny wasn't smiling.

"Is that a joke, or am I supposed to start trying to remember every Hispanic man at my gym whose first name I don't know?"

"It's a joke," I broke in. "And it's not."

Lenny turned his attention to me. "Is this an interview or a riddle off? Am I supposed to know this Arturo guy somehow?"

"If you do, it'd be because he dated Jessica."

"I have no interest in her social life. Haven't for years."

"So you don't know who she dated?"

"Not only that. I don't care if she dated the entire locker room of the New York Rangers."

"Funny," Winslow said. "I had you pegged more as an Islanders fan."

"I don't follow sports. What else do you want to know? My reading list?"

I stepped in again. "So just to be clear, you didn't know an artist named Arturo who dated Jessica?"

"No."

The Last Collar

We stood in silence for a good thirty seconds. Finally, Lenny held out his hands questioningly. "What?"

"You're hiding something. You have been all along."

"Quite possibly. There's a lot in my life that is none of your affair."

"Affair? Don't you mean business?"

"It amounts to the same thing."

"Yeah, huh?"

"Is that a question?"

I tapped my pen on my empty sheet of notepad paper, letting the silence stretch. Then I said, "Here's the thing, Leonard. This is one that will appeal to your educated side and your street side, so listen, okay?"

He glanced at his watch, then gestured for me to continue.

"We know you're hiding something, but we don't know what it is. And since we're investigating a homicide, when we don't know something, it makes us nervous. Even suspicious. So we keep pecking at a thing until we find out what it is. You feel me?"

He didn't answer, only stared at me. But I could tell he was thinking it through.

Winslow stepped in because...well, because he

was Winslow. "What he's saying, shitbird, is that we're going to keep coming back at you until we figure out what the fuck you're hiding. Get it, or do I need to write it up in a scholarly journal or some shit?"

Lenny ignored him, keeping his eyes on me.

"All I care about is solving her murder, Mr. Travis," I told him quietly. "If it doesn't have to do with this case, I really don't care what else you're into."

"Though we can probably guess," Winslow added.

Lenny stared for a few moments longer. Then he seemed to have come to a decision because his expression changed. "I had an affair," he said.

"No shit," Winslow said. "With an underage girl. You went to prison. We know."

Lenny snapped his gaze toward him. "Not *that*. And she wasn't exactly under-aged...oh, never mind. It's not going to change your mind about me." He shook his head. "While Jessica and I were married, I had an affair."

"So? People do it all the time. They even got websites for it now."

"This was a little closer to home."

"Yeah. Who?"

Lenny turned back to me. "Her sister. Morgan."

Winslow whistled. "Well, god*damn*."

Lenny excused himself. Unbidden, he called his next client and canceled their session. When he returned, he was calm and I got none of the vibe I'd sensed before that he was hiding something.

"How long?"

He shrugged. "Maybe half the time Jessica and I were together."

"Which half?"

"The second half."

"After you figured out what a fake Jessica Shannon was."

He clenched his teeth and didn't answer. The muscles at the corner of his jaw bunched and ground.

"Hey, Leonard, your words, not mine."

"It was during that time frame, yes."

"Why?"

"Lots of reasons."

"Name a few."

He ticked them off. "She was attractive. She was adventurous. She wanted it."

"There's always that," Winslow said. "A little minx too, I bet."

I understood what had spurred Winslow's comment. There was something about Morgan, a strength and purposefulness. I thought back to the time we first met her. You could just see the power in her legs as she led us into her sister's apartment. I imagined her muscular legs wrapped around me. I remembered thinking, *Yeah, boy. She looks like she can break it off.*

Lenny shrugged. "She was wild and crazy, yes. She liked sex. It was dangerous. And I was bored."

"Dangerous?" I asked. "How was she dangerous?"

He raised an eyebrow. "I was married to her sister. Fucking her was dangerous."

I got it then. "And therefore exciting."

"Exactly."

"Which cured the boredom."

"For a while. But these things that burn hot tend to flame out, don't they?"

"Is that what happened between the two of you?"

He thought about it. "I guess not, actually. I'd grown tired of Morgan but not bored enough to end it. Then I went to prison. So in a sense, it never had a defined ending."

"But it ended?"

He shrugged. "Physically, yes. But she wrote me in prison."

"She wrote you letters?" Winslow asked in mild amazement.

"Didn't I just say that?"

"How often?" I asked.

"Weekly. Sometimes more."

"What kind of letters?"

"The kind that said she loved me, missed me, and couldn't wait until I was released so we could be together."

"Did that interest you?"

"Not in the slightest. The older sister is as vacuous as the younger one, albeit for different reasons."

"Yet you banged them both," Winslow put in.

"Clearly."

"Makes for a nice story to tell at the bar, don't it?"

"If I frequented the kinds of bars where people talked about such things, perhaps."

"People talk about those kinds of things in *all* bars," Winslow said.

Lenny didn't reply.

"So you broke it off while you were still inside?" I asked.

He hesitated, then shook his head. "No."

"Why not?"

He gave me a frank look. "It pays to have someone on the outside. Someone who can bring you things, put some money on the books. Jessica rarely did. It came too close to shattering the illusion she was living that I was merely away on some sabbatical."

"When did you break it off then? Or did you?"

"Of course I did. Shortly after my release. I told her in person."

"Before or after you got your load off?" Winslow sneered.

Lenny continued to ignore him.

"How'd she take it?" I asked.

"How do they always take it?"

"You tell me."

"She was upset."

"Understandable, right? I mean, she stood by you all that time. Kept you in shower shoes and cigarettes. Must have broken her heart."

"If you say so."

"I want you to say so."

"All right. Yes, it broke her heart."

"Did you tell her the truth?"

He hesitated again. Then, "No."

"Why not?"

"Because that would've been cruel."

"Funny," Winslow said. "'Cause you strike me as such a caring soul."

"You start a lot of your sentences with that word."

"What word?"

"Funny. Only what follows never is."

Winslow pointed his finger at him and tipped him a wink. "That's what makes it funny, pal."

"What did you tell her, Leonard?" I asked.

He turned back to me. "I told her that being inside turned me gay. She was shallow enough to believe such a thing, and that was the end of it, because it was no longer a rejection of her, but of the entire female gender." He smiled humorlessly. "Not her fault, you see?"

I knew I wasn't going to get anything more of value from Lenny, and so I settled for getting Winslow out of there before he could make any more out of Lenny's last comment.

Chapter Twenty-Seven

"You believe him?" Winslow asked me in the car.

"About the sister? Of course."

"No, not that. I believe him on that one. She's a nice little piece, though not as nice as Jessica. And he is a total dog."

"Then what? The gay part?"

"No. Dude's not a homo. I get that he told her that to let her down easy. I'm not an idiot."

I raised my eyebrows at him and said nothing.

"Funny, asshole. What I mean, do you believe he's not the doer?"

I considered it. "One thing bothers me," I said, "Jessica Shannon was strangled."

"So she was."

"From behind. Not the usual way."

"Correct."

I didn't say anything.

Winslow stopped at a red light and looked over at me. "So?"

"Takes some strong hands to do that, don't you

think? The kind of strong hands that come with pumping iron?"

A slow smile spread across his face. "Yes, it would. So you like him?"

"Maybe. Take some proving, though."

"That's our job, kemosabe. You got any ideas?"

I sighed. "His alibi holds up. I don't know how to break it, if he's the doer."

Winslow's expression soured. "So you're not sure it's him? Jesus, Mocha. Make up your mind."

"I'm trying to. That's why we're investigating, dipshit."

"Dipshit? What're you, in the seventh grade?"

"Eighth." I thought about it some more. "Could still be Arturo."

"Little guy," Winslow said. He held out a hand and wiggled his fingers. "Little hands."

"True. But a little man with little hands can still be strong."

"He's a fucking *artist*, not a construction worker."

"True enough, but Lenny's a counselor. Besides, Arturo's slimier."

"You sure?" Winslow's expression was doubtful.

"What do you mean?"

"I mean," Winslow said, "that I think Lenny's

just as slimy. Maybe more so. He is just smarter about it. More...refined."

I considered that. "You're probably right."

"You should realize that more often, pal."

"What do they say about a broken clock?" I said.

"To call a clock repairman, smart ass."

"No, something about being right twice a day."

"Funny."

"You do say that a lot."

"Fuck you."

"That, too."

"Mocha, where are we going?"

I sighed. "I have no fucking idea."

Then my phone rang.

Chapter Twenty-Eight

"It's the watch commander," I announced as I read the title that had popped up on the screen. Judging by the time of day Mike Reardon was on duty and would be on the line when I answered. "Wonder what this is about?" I hit the Accept button. "Moccia."

"Johnny M, what's shaking?" he asked in his regular jovial voice.

"Nicki Minaj's giant twerking ass cheeks."

He snorted on the other end of the line. "Cut it out, Mocha, you'll give me a heart attack."

A fresh call popped up on the screen with a 415 area code. Yup. It was Sandra, no doubt calling to tear me a fresh one. I suddenly remembered the check I was sup-posed to put in the mail. I hadn't purposely neglected to send it, but what with the grim reaper's hand on my shoulder and all, I'd just forgotten to write it out. Guilt surfaced at the same time as my revelation. I could hear Dr. Stiviak's irksome voice in my ear telling me to get my priorities straight, to make things right with my family and to reconnect with Sophia. Worst of all, the man was right and I just hated being wrong. I didn't want to let the call go to voicemail but there was no choice. Her timing was shitty and I'd just have to call back Her Majesty, the Queen of Broken Stones, at my first opportunity or maybe my second.

Reardon's timing was even shittier than Sandra's. I barked at him, "So what's going on, Mike, you've got time to kill or do you have something valuable to tell me?"

"Geez, what a grouch. I figured you'd be happy to hear from me."

"Not unless you've got make-my-day-type information to pass along. Coltrane's three molars deep into my bony Italian keester, so tell me something that will make me smile."

"Okay, Mr. Personality," he began in a sober voice. "Pull your pad and pen out of the Crackerjack box and write this down—Eighteen Little West Twelfth Street. Ring a bell, shit for brains?"

The address did ring a bell, not so much a giant clanging Notre Dame cathedral bell but one of those dainty little Swiss bell, the one's the yodelers wear on their lederhosen. There was something vaguely familiar about the address but my chemical cocktail-saturated brain couldn't put its finger on it, and Reardon's "shit for brains" crack just downright pissed me off more than I already was. I allowed myself a half-moment to wallow in self-pity before blurting, "Just fucking tell me already."

Winslow's jaw dropped.

Way to go, John. You jerk!

"A Tout le Monde, ass bag. You and Winslow were there the other day, remember? A tip came in from someone named Camille about that douchebag Arturo Calderas you were looking for."

"Oh yeah. Right."

"Jesus, what a prick," he muttered. "We just got a call, an altercation broke out during a showing and I figured...you know what? Fuck you, Mocha. Figure it out yourself." The line went dead.

Winslow gaped at me. "Jesus, John, what the hell? Reardon's one of the good ones. You all right, buddy?"

For a moment I thought about telling Winslow that the next time he saw me I'd probably be horizontal in a box wearing face makeup, but the timing was wrong. It was too soon to suit my purpose so I just sold the big fella the most convenient lie. "Yeah. Shit. Sandra was calling in and I let it go to voicemail. I forgot to mail her the child support money I neglected to mail the first of the month."

He grimaced. "Mocha, what's wrong with you? You don't care if your daughter has food in her belly? I know Sandra can be a witch but it's not like you to forget about your own kid. Shit, she's only four."

I held up a flat hand to shield myself from Winslow's onslaught. "Yeah. Yeah. I know. I'm a great big steaming pile of sheep shit. What can I say? I've got a lot on my goddamn mind."

"You're all over the place, man. If I didn't know better I'd say you had 'roid rage. You trying to bulk up or something?"

"Like I might ever take PEDs." I should've apologized for my hot temper but my emotional fire extinguisher was completely discharged. Instead, I switched gears. "Reardon says there's an altercation at the gallery Arturo is holed up at. Let's check it out."

Chapter Twenty-Nine

Once upon a time David Brenner joked that on one of his early trips to the Big Apple, a water main exploded sending a manhole cover a hundred feet into the air atop the zenith of a mighty geyser. He watched in awe as the heavy steel plate flipped end over end in the air, and just before it hit the ground a New York bystander called out, "Heads."

In that vein, the unflappable New York art enthusiasts who had been chased from A Tout le Monde were loitering about, wine glasses in hand, chatting as if nothing had happened.

Winslow and I pushed through the crowd and went up the steps. Aside from staff and two patrolmen the gallery was empty. The massive canvases that hung on the wall were a study in black and white. Red wine had stained the walls and the à la Jackson Pollock paintings, which in my opinion made the exhibit far more interesting. Shards of glass from fractured wine glasses littered the clear maple floors.

"And they say it takes talent to paint," Winslow snickered. "I could do the same thing with a gallon of Benjamin Moore and a kid's Super Soaker."

"Yes, of course, what a shame the art world never stumbled across the mind-blowing talent that is you." I slapped his arm with the back of my hand. "Come on, Rembrandt, the light's on in Dani's office."

With his square head and fat face Dani Klemperer looked like a come-to-life version of Mr. Stay Puft, the marshmallow man. His eyes were closed and his head-phones were in place. The only thing louder than the music bleeding from his headphones was his Vesuvius red jumpsuit. I could tell from the beat that the diehard Rush fan was bobble-heading to the beat of "Limelight."

Winslow tapped him on the shoulder. He clutched his chest and pried his Sennheisers off his ears. He blurted, "Jesus, Mary, and Joseph Stalin. You startled me."

"Mr. Klemperer, I'm Detective Winslow and this is Detective Moccia."

He seemed startled. "Detectives?"

"Yes," Winslow replied. "We were here the other day."

"No you weren't. I remember everyone who

steps foot in my gallery."

"Everyone who steps foot in your gallery when your eyes are open."

"Oh! I'm mortified. The music—I get lost in it, but since when is embarrassment a crime?" he chuckled.

"It's not. Want to tell us what went on here?" Winslow asked.

"Honestly, it was nothing," he said with a dismissive wave of the hand. "My boyfriend threw a hissy fit and started tossing wine glasses like they were water balloons."

"We noticed," Winslow said. "Added a little color to your black and white exhibit."

"A vast improvement," Klemperer chortled.

"This boyfriend of yours wouldn't happen to be Arturo Calderas, would it?"

"Oh, heavens. What's he done now? He's not turning tricks again, is he? I told him I'd throw him out on his fine Latino behind if he did." His eyebrows peaked. "Camille caught him once you know. He was in the bathroom giving a blowie to the District Attorney."

Winslow's jaw dropped. "Vance Linwood?"

"Uh-huh," he confirmed with a double head nod.

I didn't know why Winslow was surprised.

Linwood was an old queen and everyone knew it. Everyone except Winslow, it seemed. "Mind telling us why Arturo was so upset?"

He looked Winslow up and down. "My, but you're a tall drink of water." He patted his leg. "Sit down right here and I'll tell you all about it."

It looked like Winslow wanted to run away. He cleared his throat. "That's inappropriate, Mr. Klemperer."

He gazed at Winslow with soft eyes. "Call me Dani."

"Please continue," I said coming to my partner's rescue. "Arturo was angry. Let's focus there, shall we?"

"He's such a child. It's the same thing over and over."

"Which is?"

"He wants a showing for his work."

"Is he using his relationship with you as leverage?" Winslow asked.

"Well, of course he is but all the ass in the world isn't going to make that happen."

"Why not?"

"Well first of all, it's sculpture. Do you know what it costs to transport that kind of work? Paintings are a snap—my men go over and stack them in the van. But heavy sculpture? It takes three times the manpower and if they hit a pothole...Oh dear God, there's hell to pay." He opened his drawer and picked up an emery board. "And secondly, his shit sucks. He thinks he's using me? *Hah?* I don't think so. For the love of Pete, the man sculpts in marble. There's no interest in that kind of thing anymore. Does he think we're still in the Renaissance? Marble sculpture went out with Michelangelo."

"So you were never going to give a showing?" Winslow asked.

"Not in this gallery. His tush may go round and round like a gyroscope but it's not going to pay for all the damage he caused out there tonight. Thank God I have a top-drawer insurance policy. What a shame—all that precious art wasted."

"You mean those skid marks on the wall?"

"Yes. Those skid marks on the wall. It may be crap but that crap pays the rent."

"And where is Mr. Calderas now?" Winslow asked.

He shrugged. "Frankly, my dear, I don't give a damn where he went."

I smiled at his Rhett Butler imitation. "Now let's forget that Arturo's been a bad boy and concentrate on helping the two strapping police officers standing in front of you."

Winslow seemed taken aback. His expression read, *Are you nuts?*

Klemperer batted his eyelashes at me. "You know, I've got a leg for each of you. Sure you fellas don't want to get dirty?"

"Inappropriate," Winslow reminded him.

"So where might we find Mr. Calderas?" I asked.

He shrugged. "I don't know but you could try The Monster. It's in the West Village. That's where I met him. Or he might try to score quick coin to cover a night's hotel stay. If that's the case he usually hangs around outside Hunk-O-Mania waiting for a randy queer to pick up."

"Thank you, Mr. Klemperer. You've been enormously helpful."

"I'll show you enormous," he bantered playfully. "Are you sure you boys don't want to have a party? My lovers tell me I'm two tons of fun."

I'll bet you are. I had to bite my lip as an imprint of my obituary materialized in my mind, "Giovanni Anthony Moccia: Decorated Veteran NYC detective. Passed away suddenly while engaged in debauchery with the Stay Puft Marshmallow Man." I'd participated in all manner of depraved sex acts during my many days, but sticking a skewer in Mr. Stay Puft wasn't going to be one of them. Even a man with scarce time to complete the items on his bucket list has to draw the line somewhere.

Speaking of depraved acts, the woman I'd done things with you wouldn't attempt with a farm animal was calling again. Yes, it was Sandra, the mother of my child. I excused myself and headed for the street. I could feel my sphincter tighten even before I even heard the shrill sound of her voice.

Chapter Thirty

"I'm going back to court," she barked before I had the chance to greet her. "I'm sick and tired of chasing you month after month. Do you think this is fun for me? Trust me, I'd just as soon not talk to you at all. Ever!"

"Don't do that, Sandra. It was an oversight."

"It's bad enough that you have nothing to do with your daughter. Can't you at least be financially responsible?"

"I am financially responsible. I'm just buried," I said for my own cynical amusement. "And the reason I don't see my kid is because you moved her three thousand goddamn miles away. You've made it awfully inconvenient for me to be a good father, but it doesn't mean that I don't love my daughter." My blood pressure was jumping and I could feel the pulsing of another monster headache despite all the medication I'd been given. The beast was rising again and he was angry. "Look, I'll send out two checks by Fed Ex tomorrow morning, the late one and the one due on the first of next month, too. You'll have them the next day."

"Yeah?"

"Yeah. I just said so, didn't I?"

"You say a lot of shit."

"I've never missed a payment, Sandra. Have I been late? Yeah, but when I do it's unintentional."

"All right, I'll give you two more days but if I don't get the Fed Ex delivery I'm going straight to my attorney. Do you understand me?"

"Sure. Make the attorney rich. What do you care? It's coming out of my pocket."

"Then give me a choice, John."

"Yeah. Yeah. Yeah," I bellyached. "I get you." I shook my head, then drew a deep breath. "Hey, Sandy—"

"Sandra," she reminded me, cutting me off at the knees.

"Remember when we used to get along?"

"Not really," she snapped. "All I remember is a summer of hot fucking followed by nine months of gestation followed by years of pain and suffering. That's how I remember you, John. I bit the apple and I've been getting fucked for it ever since."

"Think we can ever get past that?"

She was silent for a moment, then, "What do you mean by 'get past it?' You mean can we ever be together again? Not likely. You smoking crack or something?"

I wish I were. "No. I mean 'get past it' as in just getting along—for Sophia's sake. I've been thinking that a visit is way overdue. It would be easier if we weren't spewing venom at each other."

"That's a hell of a lot easier said than done. I've known you almost exactly five years out of which five percent was lust and ninety-five percent was sheer unadulterated aggravation."

"So better than most marriages."

She snorted. I was surprised that she'd broken form to indulge in a laugh. I had no idea when Winslow and I would close the Jessica Shannon homicide case, but there were only scant days left before Dr. Stiviak's deadline hit, and after that...well let's just say that taking PTO wouldn't be a problem. "You going to be around next weekend? I thought—"

"Why? You thought you'd crush your daughter again by telling her you were coming out and then cancelling at the last minute?"

"That only happened once."

"Twice!"

"Look, whatever. I mean it this time. There's been some stuff going on and I really need to see the two of you."

"What kind of stuff? You getting kicked off the job or something?" she asked with concern. For the moment the malicious guttersnipe was gone and she actually sounded sympathetic, although at the heart of her compassion I knew she was strictly concerned with my ability to meet her payment schedule.

"I'd rather not discuss it over the phone. So what do you say? Next weekend okay for you? I'll book a flight and put in for time off."

"What about your cases? You sure you're not going to blow us off again?"

"Not a chance, Sandra. Short of Armageddon, nothing will keep me from getting on that plane. Can we call a truce?"

She was slow to reply. "Send me the checks and then we'll talk."

"Fair enough."

I disconnected from Sandra and looked up the number of my attorney. The clock was ticking down and I had precious little time to put my affairs in order.

Chapter Thirty-One

Winslow met me on the sidewalk. "Everything okay?"

"Yeah, fine."

He peered at me closer. "You don't look like it was fine. Was that Coltrane?"

"No."

"Well, I know it wasn't the Ghost, unless he was calling to check to see if the coast is clear. So who was it?"

I rubbed the bridge of my nose. "Sandra," I admitted.

"Oh." He hesitated, then clapped me lightly on the shoulder. "She busting your balls again? Over what this time?"

He asked his question in a curious tone. On the surface, it was all "concern for the partner" but I could hear the undercurrent that was there, too. He didn't say so most of the time, but he didn't approve of my fathering skills any more than my parents did.

"Yeah, some." Then I shrugged. "I forgot to send her a check, but we worked it out."

"Good. Get it sent. Your little girl needs shoes, right?"

"Or something."

"You need to go by the bank?" Winslow asked. "We can make the time."

"Tomorrow. I'll FedEx it tomorrow."

Winslow nodded, accepting that, but his eyes never left me. "What else?"

"Nothing."

"Bullshit."

"Really, nothing."

"Mocha, we gonna stand here for the next ten minutes going back and forth like this, or are you just going to tell me what it is so we can get back to working the case?"

He was right. He'd just keep at me like a pit bull, pestering me so I couldn't concentrate, until I told him. "I'm going to take some time. Fly out and see Sophia."

Winslow was silent for a few seconds, then he nodded approvingly and gave me another clap on the shoulder. "That'll be good for you. Both of you."

"Yeah. I know." I popped open the car door and slid into the front seat.

As Winslow dropped his bulk into the driver's seat, my phone rang.

I glanced down at the screen.

"Forensics," I told Winslow. Then I punched the button. "Moccia."

"John? It's Henry Attredge."

"Whattaya got, Hank? Please tell me it's DNA."

"Sorry, no. But something in the autopsy that I thought you might want to be aware of."

"Go ahead."

"The victim was strangled from behind, as you know. The injury pattern supports this, particularly the bruises caused by the suspect's fingers."

"So?"

"So, I know you're trying to narrow the suspect field on this. That's why I reviewed the measurements of the bruises, and did a little comparison."

"Against what?"

"Against the average. I wondered if it would be helpful to know if your suspect had big hands or not."

A small splash of cold shock lit up my lower belly.

Shit.

I should have thought of this.

And then my next thought came.
Big hands.
Lenny, you son of a bitch.
"What did you find out?"
"Your guy did *not* have big hands."
"He didn't?" My visions of slapping cuffs on Lenny turned into smoke. "Are you sure?"
"I'm certain. In fact, your guy has hands that are considerably smaller than average."
"No shit."
"None. Does that help at all?"
"It does. Thanks, Hank."
"Anytime."
I hung up. This felt like the first real lead in a long while.
"What is it?" Winslow asked.
"Our killer has small hands," I told him.
"Yeah, huh?"
"Yeah. He has small, *strong* hands."
Winslow's face lit up. "Like a sculptor?"
"Exactly like that."
Winslow had an *I'm proud of myself* smile on his face. "Here's a present for you, dick wad." He reached into his shirt pocket, withdrew a yellow sticky note, and pasted it on my shoulder.
An address was scribbled on it. It wasn't Winslow's handwriting. "I was expecting a gold

star."

"For being father of the year? Yeah. Dream on."

"So what's with the address?"

"It's a storage locker where Arturo stores his shitty marble sculptures. Dani volunteered the address."

"Well then hot damn," I muttered. "Let's go find Arturo."

Chapter Thirty-Two

"So what are you gonna do after you clock out for the last time?" I asked.

Winslow turned his gaze from the road and stared at me with a strange expression. It probably wasn't the question itself as much as the desperation he must've heard in my voice that prompted, "Are you sure you're all right, John?"

"Of course I'm all right. What kind of question is that?"

"No, seriously—there's something going on with you. Something is wrong and you're trying to cover it up."

I'd made a career of busting Winslow's balls but there was no denying that he was a seasoned detective with strong instincts and I wondered just how long I could go on bullshitting the man. Stiviak's deadline was looming. *Just a few more days, I suppose. The walls of Jericho are about to come crashing down.*

And then they did.

A feeling of hopelessness washed over me like a tidal wave of grief. I felt the muscles in my face constrict as an ache swarmed in my gut. My uncle used to tell me that he had a "low feeling" in his belly. The expression used to puzzle me but I came to realize it was the way he described his depression. It took less than a split-second for me to understand how he felt. It was horrible, far worse than the reality of my impending death.

Knock it off, I told myself. *This isn't you.*

I could sense Winslow staring at me. He didn't say a word, but he turned the wheel sharply and pulled to the curb. He popped out of the car and rescued a bottle of water from his stash in the trunk. "What's wrong, John? Do you need a doctor?"

I bit my lip and shook my head side to side.

Winslow opened the bottle and handed it to me.

I wet my lips and turned to him, wanting to tell him but unable to find the words.

"John, why are you acting so squirrely? Whatever it is, it'll be all right."

"Gonna beat you to the punch, my friend. Gonna pull the pin."

His face screwed up in confusion. "But you haven't put in your twenty yet. You've still got two years—" Suddenly, the confusion melted away. He hadn't finished the sentence but already had it figured out. "How bad?"

"Book a flight to San Diego bad. Spill your guts to your partner bad."

Winslow's chest heaved and his expression saddened. "Jesus, John, cancer?"

I tapped my temple. "Glioma. Explains a lot, right? Sorry I didn't tell you right away, but I needed for Sophia and Sandra to get survivor's benefits and...I guess that was pretty selfish. I could've put you in danger."

He shook his head rapidly. "Christ. I don't know what to say."

"Say you'll keep your mouth shut until the end of the week. It'll give us a little more time to wrap up the case. I'll tell Coltrane at the end of the shift on Friday."

"Did you tell anyone on the squad?"

"No. I just told my folks."

"Yesterday's big lunch?"

I nodded.

He sighed. "Like you said, it explains a lot." He stared at me and I could see him misting up. "Just couldn't deal with a new partner, could you?"

"Take it easy, ya big lug. I'm not ready for the long goodbye...not today anyhow."

"How long have you known?"

"Couple months. The doc didn't know how fast it was growing but I paid Allison a booty call the other night and lost my shit right in front of her. Spent the night in the hospital and found out that the tumor had grown like a motherfucker—went straight from the hospital to the Italian deli and then told my parents."

"So Sandra doesn't know."

"Not yet. I'll tell her in person."

"And all the while she's busting your shoes about child support money. I don't know how you kept quiet."

"Apples and oranges, my friend. There's no love in our relationship but she'll still have to bring up Sophia as a single mother. I'm just hoping she lets her stay close with my folks. She's been good about that up to now."

"I can't see why that would change."

"Three thousand miles—I hope she'll come to New York a couple times a year. I'm going to ask her to anyway. With my savings, insurance, and death benefits they should be okay for a long time."

A long silent moment passed. I guess neither of us knew what to say. "So what now?" he asked.

"Well if I can buy forty-eight hours of silence we just go back to work."

"Are you feeling well enough to..."

"Yeah, the doc loaded me up on a ton of meds. I can hold my own for a couple of days." He was looking weepy again. "What about you? Are you sure you can hold it together? I don't want you fucking up my unusually short life expectancy."

He seemed thoughtful for a moment, then, "Okay." He cranked the engine. "IPS?"

"Yup. Important Police Shit. Let's go jack up light-fingers Arturo."

His expression brightened and then he snorted. "Mocha, you bastard, I still can't believe you banged Allison."

Chapter Thirty-Three

"What do you think we'd find if we opened up all of these storage units, Mocha?"

"I don't know, useless shit, illegal shit, cash, drugs, worn women's panties...all kinds of treasures." The storage complex was an old converted factory building in Washington Heights with a view of the George Washington Bridge. The windows had been bricked up. The exterior walls were covered with graffiti, not artistic work, but crappy vandal spray painting. The kinds of masterpieces bored kids were responsible for. Apparently these particular kids were colorblind.

Winslow checked the time. "The Ghost is supposed to swing by with a warrant."

"Smart money says he dumps the chore on someone else. You know if I'm lucky I may never see the scarce SOB again."

Winslow shrugged in a manner that suggested I hadn't been all that lucky.

The woman behind the reception glass was a

The Last Collar

shrew named Mary Ellen who greeted us as if we were contagious Ebola patients. Dani had provided Winslow with the address of the storage facility but not the number of Arturo's storage unit. Winslow provided ID and gave her the scoop on our investigation to which she responded, "Got a warrant?"

"Yes. It's on the way," he replied.

"So is Christmas." She checked the clock on the wall. "I clock out in eleven minutes. I hope whomever is on the way stops for a cup of coffee so that you two can be someone else's pain in the ass."

"The City of New York appreciates your cooperation, ma'am. Where's your broom parked? We'll stick around to make sure you're safely airborne." I flipped her the finger.

"Very professional," she griped.

"Go home and stir the cauldron, lady." I walked off.

Winslow followed. "Gonna level a few trees on your way out of town?"

"Who? Her? Trust me, Winslow, I held back. People like her are all attitude. I'd like to see what this city would be like without NYPD."

"You're not going to change that, buddy, and neither am I—not in the next two days anyway."

"Yeah. I know. It just irks me." We walked outside, away from the stale air and dust. It was one of those sublime nights, low humidity and a breeze that was just downright sexy. "Maybe I'll take up smoking."

"Can't believe I'm about to say this but, yeah. Why not? Try a goddamn hookah if you like."

"Guess I could try all kinds of crazy shit now, skydiving, spelunking, cliff diving. I mean, might as well, right?"

"Sure. Put together a quick bucket list and go crazy. Hell, I'll do it with you."

"You mean like Jack Nicholson and Morgan Freeman?"

"Something like that, but go see your kid first—not the other way round."

A car pulled up so stealthily that I didn't notice it until it had come to a stop.

"Jesus Christ," Winslow announced. "I don't believe it. It's Gastineau. It's the fucking Ghost."

"You were saying...about my luck?"

Gastineau left the motor running and got out of the car. He seemed to drift above the ground like the apparition he was named for. I hit the stopwatch button on my Casio G-Shock. "To what do we owe this para-normal pleasure?"

Gastineau ignored me and handed Winslow the

warrant. "The El Tee wants a report, first thing. You two fine officers plan on swinging by the station house for coffee and crullers in the morning?"

"We'll think about it," I said flippantly.

"Think about it all you want, Mocha. Come roll call, Coltrane will be hemorrhaging blood from his eyeballs if two of you aren't there front and center."

"The El Tee needs a prescription for Xanax."

"He also needs Kevlar shorts to keep the Chief of Ds from crawling up his ass." He turned back to the car. "See you first thing, gentlemen. Good luck with your search."

The Ghost dropped in behind the wheel and sped away.

"What do you think?" Winslow asked.

I hit the stopwatch button for the second time and showed Winslow the elapsed time digital readout. "Fifty-eight seconds. He set a new record."

Chapter Thirty-Four

The Wicked Witch of the West flipped me the bird as she hit the streets and disappeared into the subway. She'd been replaced by a smallish fellow named Hector, who looked up Arturo's locker number without so much as asking to see the warrant. He escorted us to the storage unit, used a master key to unlock it, and dropped the opened padlock into Winslow's massive palm.

"He was helpful."

"Compared to the harpy he replaced, syphilis is helpful."

He chuckled. "True dat."

I lifted the shutter-style door. The unit was more than a storage locker. It was Arturo's studio, a compact work space replete with blocks of marble, finished works, and stone cutting tools. To my eye his work wasn't at all bad. The details of the eyes and all of the most delicate features seemed expertly crafted. Arturo's work might not have had important commercial value but it was evident to

The Last Collar

a layperson that the man was quite talented.

"I hate to give that prick Arturo mad props but this stuff isn't half-bad."

I examined his workbench upon which a woman's bust stood partially completed. The tools of his trade, the hammers, chisels, and files rested haphazardly about.

"What's this?" Winslow called out. He approached holding a tube of ointment and a wastepaper basket. "Voltaren Gel," he said as he handed me the tube. He poked around in the trash pail with his glove-covered hand. He showed me discarded packaging for the gel and two empty tubes. "Whatever it is, he uses a lot of it."

I picked up an empty packet and found the insert still inside. I unfolded it and read the section marked *Indication and Usage*. "Voltaren Gel is indicated for the relief of the pain of osteoarthritis of joints amenable to topical treatment, such as the knees and those of the hands."

I glanced up at Winslow.

"Looks like you were right—Arturo had all the hand strength necessary to strangle Jessica from behind. The sculpting must have made his hands very strong. He probably uses this topical anti-inflammatory to sooth his aching hands."

"I'll bet he gave an amazing rub and tug,"

Winslow chuckled.

An old metal desk was pushed up against the back wall. I sat down in the desk chair and tried the drawers. They were locked. I used one of Arturo's chisels to pry each of the drawers open. There was nothing remarkable in the top drawers but in one of the lower folder drawers... "Hey, Winslow," I cried out. "Get a look at—"

"Holy shit!" he blurted.

The drawer was filled to the top with bundles of hundred-dollar bills.

Chapter Thirty-Five

"How much?" Winslow asked.

I finished stacking the bills on top of the old metal desk. "It looks like he bundled them twenty-five to a stack, so twenty-five hundred dollars per bundle." I started counting the number of bundles.

"Twenty-five times one hundred is twenty-five hundred? Wow, that's high concept math, Good Will Hunting."

I gave him the finger with my left without breaking stride counting with my right. I was glad Winslow kept the same ol', same ol' coming with how we communicated. Not only did it keep me in the game, but it kept me from thinking about what waited for me just around the corner.

Then again, maybe it was just habit.

I finished counting. "Thirty-three bundles, so...how much is that?"

"About a hundred dollars," Winslow deadpanned in his best Rainman voice.

"Close. But I get...eighty-two thousand, five

hundred."

Winslow whistled softly.

"It doesn't make sense," I said. "Eighty two large he's got stockpiled here. But all the while, he's crying poverty and sponging off people. To what end?"

"To spend their money, not his."

"Sure, but why is he saving this? What's his end game?"

"Not everyone has one, Mocha. Sometimes people just save money."

I shook my head. "No, not this guy. He's got a plan. We just don't know what it is yet."

"Eighty-two," Winslow mused quietly. "That's a year's salary for a lot of people."

I glanced at him. "Not you?"

"Shit," he grinned. "I get more overtime than you ever dreamed. I pick up those dead shifts all the time. I was well north of six figures last year."

"Too bad you didn't spend some of it on your wardrobe." I picked one of the bundles and waved it. "Somehow I don't think Arturo got this covering shifts for other sculptors."

Winslow snorted. "He got it scamming people like Dani."

"Or Jessica Shannon."

He thought about it. "Yeah, maybe. But why

kill her? I mean, you've got a golden goose, you don't wring its neck, right?"

"Maybe she decided to quit paying."

"Quit? Why was she paying in the first place?" Winslow shook his head. "It doesn't make sense. Even if it was a honey pot scam or some kind of blackmail, why kill her when it ends? A guy like Arturo, you figure he'd just chalk it up, walk away, and find the next mark. Eighty large isn't chump change, but it isn't change-your-life money. Why kill her?"

"I don't know," I admitted. "But let's look at what we've got."

He gave me a *go ahead* gesture. "Make your case, Sherlock."

"We know Arturo and Jessica dated."

"And broke up," Winslow added.

"Sure. But they dated. And we know that Arturo's motivation is at least largely centered around money, which Jessica has."

"Had."

I ignored his correction. "We know she was murdered, strangled from behind by someone with small, strong hands." I made a sweeping motion around the room. "And we know Arturo has small, strong hands."

Winslow shook his head. "No D.A. will charge

murder on that. It's all circumstantial."

"Arturo lied to us, too."

"Still circumstantial. And even if we find DNA or prints or anything else at the vic's residence, any first year public defender can cast reasonable doubt on that. They dated, remember? So of course there'd be evidence of his presence in the apartment."

"Are you trying to make this case or destroy it?" I asked, but I didn't mean it. He was doing what he was supposed to do—poke holes in my theory.

"I'm being kind compared to what the D.A. will say, and you know it. Now, you got any more to go on?"

I thought about it. "Let's pick up Arturo."

"And do what? He's lawyered up, so we can't talk to him without his attorney present."

"I don't want to talk to him."

Winslow gave me a confused look. I didn't answer. And then, just like when he figured out what was going on with my health, he came to the same conclusion I had. "We get a warrant and forensics takes exact measurements of his hands. Then we see if they can match those measurements up to the injury pattern."

I cocked a finger and thumb gun at him and dropped the thumb, firing. "You got it."

"It's a long shot," he said, "but it's better than anything else we've got. I still want to know what he's doing with all this cash."

I shrugged. "Maybe when he finds out we've seized it, he'll feel the need to identify the source of these funds. And if he hasn't paid taxes on said funds..."

Winslow smiled, "We've got him on an Al Capone charge. Income tax evasion." He nodded, obviously encouraged. "That's a hell of a lever to take into the interview room."

"What about his attorney?" I asked, my tone mocking.

"Oh, I think he'll forget about that as soon as he sees thirty-two bundles of green love dancing away toward the evidence facility. Somehow, I think he'll want to have a conversation about that, without a suit in the room."

I thought so, too.

Chapter Thirty-Six

I counted the money again, bagged it up, and labeled it. While I filled in the forms, Winslow wandered around the small, makeshift studio. He stopped at the incomplete bust of a woman on a pedestal.

"You've got to be kidding me," he said, his voice stunned.

I looked up.

"No way," he murmured.

"What is it?"

He pointed at the bust. "Did you look at this?"

"Yeah, so?"

"I mean, did you really look? Can't you see the resemblance? It's her."

"Her?"

"Yeah," he said. "*Her*. Jessica."

I stood and walked over to check it out. The bust was far from complete, and much of the surface was still rough and ill-defined, but I could see what Winslow meant, at least in the most general of ways. The sculpture had the same general shape and contour of Jessica Shannon's features, but it wasn't an exact replica by any means.

"See it?"

"Sorta," I admitted. "But it's pretty thin."

"Says the guy who just ran an anorexic case past me?" He pointed at her forehead, jaw, and cheeks. "Look there, there, and there. It's bang on."

I looked, then shrugged. "I see your point." I reached out and patted the unfinished sculpture on the head. "At the least, she'll bear a family resemblance when he's finished. No changing that now."

Winslow sighed. "If you were the one who figured it out, this would suddenly be a major clue. But I found it, so it's 'thin.'"

"Don't pout. It makes you look older."

"Get your little bags of money, smart ass. Let's go find our killer."

"So you're convinced now, huh?"

"You don't have to convince me, Mocha. You gotta make Coltrane believe, and more importantly, the D.A. And you know what would really amp up his 'I believe' factor?"

"Gospel music?"

"Funny, but no."

"Then what?"

He grinned. "A confession."

We drove with the evidence bag full of money on the console between us. I wondered if Winslow was thinking about how much of that cash Arturo really needed. A few of those bundles would go a ways toward his kids' college funds. Buy a few of their textbooks.

Or Sophia's, for that matter.

Not for the first time, I wished I was that kind of cop, but I wasn't, and a tumor wasn't going to change that.

"Where to?" Winslow asked.

"I don't know. The gallery?"

"I'd say he burned that bridge."

"Probably." A thought occurred to me. I pulled out my notebook and dialed the number of Dani's gallery.

"A Tout le Monde," a woman answered.

"Camille?"

"Speaking."

"This is Detective Moccia, NYPD. We're trying to locate Arturo Calderas. Any ideas?"

Silence. Then, "I thought you had him already."

"We did, but we couldn't charge him, so he

walked. Now we have something else we want to talk to him about. Do you have any idea where he might be staying?"

"No."

"He's not there, is he?"

"No, thankfully." The disgust was plain in her voice.

I thought about Camille, and about Dani, and I realized I'd made some assumptions on our visit to the gallery about who she had feelings for that I figured weren't too far off. Unrequited love, and all those other clichés, but clichés get that way by being at least partially true some of the time. Only in this case, I was pretty sure I'd guessed wrong about the target of Camille's unreturned affection. Either way, it was a safe bet she wasn't going to protect Arturo on Dani's behalf or anyone else's, for that matter.

"Any suggestions on where I could try?"

"How about the local snake pit?"

I thanked her and hung up, then looked over at Winslow and shrugged. "It was worth a try."

"Try the sister. Morgan. She might know something."

"Might as well, since we're grasping at straws anyway." I found Morgan's number and dialed. After six rings, it went to voicemail. I almost hung up, then decided to leave a message. I repeated what I'd told Camille a few moments ago, then hung up. "Who else?"

Winslow considered. "What about the art guy?"

"Dani?"

"Yeah. He might have an idea the secretary didn't or that he didn't have earlier. Them being *luv-vers* and all."

I thought about it, then figured what the hell and called Camille back. Dani wasn't in but she promised to give him the message and have him call if he knew anything.

After I hung up, I gave Winslow a forlorn look. "That's all I got, partner. I am tapped. How about you?"

"Tapped and run dry," he agreed.

I glanced at my watch. "I'll call in a pickup order on Arturo, in case a uniform or some other detective comes across him."

"Sounds good."

"You wanna drop me off at my place? We'll go at this again in the morning."

"Nope."

"Huh?"

He looked over at me. "You're coming to dinner tonight."

The Last Collar

"Matt—"

"No arguing."

I was quiet for a minute. As much as I was tired and wanted to sleep, his offer sounded good. Being around people sounded good. In the morning, Coltrane was going to climb our asses again, and maybe Arturo would still be in the wind. Even if we got him picked up, it was no way a sure thing that my theory would hold water, and Coltrane would be sure to let me know. I wasn't looking forward to any of that, but the idea of a nice dinner with the Winslow family?

I could get behind that.

"Sure, partner," I said. "No arguing."

Chapter Thirty-Seven

Dinner at the Winslow house was the most normal thing I've ever experienced in my life. The whole family was right out of a family TV show. Not perfect or any-thing, but lots of love in the house.

Winslow was a different person around his family. The edge in his personality he carried at work disappeared, and he became Winnie the Pooh. Every once in a while, when a tiny bit of Work Winslow would crop up while he was talking to me, Sarah would give him a gentle reprimand—sometimes only a glance, and Work Winslow would go away and Pooh Bear would come back.

It was sickly sweet in some ways, especially compared to my bachelor lifestyle. But it also gave me an inkling of what I'd missed out on with Sandra and Sophia. And goddamned if I didn't soak in every moment, and enjoy every bite. I even had seconds.

Afterwards, Winslow offered me a beer. We sat

The Last Collar

in his backyard and sipped from the bottles. He didn't say anything for a long time. Finally, without looking at me, he said, "You're the best partner I ever had, John. The best."

His voice was thick, and I didn't trust myself to answer him, so I just raised my bottle to him. He caught my movement with his peripheral vision and clinked my bottle without looking my way.

We drank.

Afterwards, we came back inside for some dessert. Sarah made some gluten-free, vegan carrot cake. I expected it to taste like straw and chalk dust, but it was actually pretty good.

I told her it was the best I'd ever had. She looked at me, a little surprised, but said thanks.

Winslow offered me the fold-out bed in the living room, but I begged off. I wanted to sleep in my own bed, and wake up in my own place. He tossed me the keys to the car and said I could pick him up in the morning.

"Parking is a bitch at my place," I said, throwing them back. "Just drop me off."

Even though it was a thirty-minute drive to my place, and so an hour round trip for him, he agreed without complaint. I felt a little guilty, since I knew the reason for it, but in the end, I said to hell with it. Parking did suck in my neighborhood, and

Winslow's house had a nice wide driveway.

I also knew Sarah would ask him questions when he got back, because she was a better detective than either one of us. She'd picked up on something, and my guess was she'd have it out of Winslow before he hung his keys on the rack near the door that was in the shape of an octopus, with key pegs on every tentacle.

He drove me home. Neighborhoods with houses that had driveways and backyards gave way to houses with small front yards or no yards at all. Those eventually gave way to urban streets with businesses and apartments only. All in the span of a thirty-minute drive.

He stopped in front of my building. "See you in the morning, partner."

"Yeah. Prepare for the Coltrane Express."

He smiled.

"What?" I asked.

"Nothing. I just had an epiphany, is all."

"You just banged a stripper named Tiffany?"

"No. An epiphany. A sudden understanding."

"I know what it means. I'm surprised *you* know the word."

"I get the word of the day on Facebook. 'Epiphany' was last Tuesday's word."

"You're on Facebook?"

"Everyone's on Facebook."

"Which is why no one is on Facebook."

"Huh?"

"Never mind. What's your epiphany?"

"Oh." He smiled again. "Just that Coltrane can yell all he wants and it don't mean nothing, because I'm alive and well, and I'm going to make my pension in less than seven months. And you...well, he can't touch you any more, even if he wanted to."

I nodded slowly. "You're right."

"I know."

"How's it feel?"

"How's what feel?"

"Being right for the first time?"

He scowled. "Mocha..."

"They say the first time is the best, you know."

"Get out of my car."

I opened the door and stepped out. "Good night, Matt. And thanks."

He nodded in understanding. "See you in the morning."

I closed the door, and he drove away.

I let myself into my apartment, and grabbed a beer from the fridge. I'd intended on taking a shower, and maybe watching some TV before I crashed. But as I sipped the beer, I wandered into the bedroom and sat on the edge of the bed. I kicked off my shoes, put my gun and badge on the nightstand, and laid back to look at the ceiling.

I was asleep before I knew it.

Chapter Thirty-Eight

I woke up in the same position the next morning, my hand still curled around the now warm beer. I rose, poured it down the bathroom drain, and got into the shower.

I managed to get cleaned up and dressed before my cell phone buzzed with a text from Winslow that he was waiting downstairs. That was when I noticed I had a voice message. I must have slept through the call last night.

Once dressed, I headed downstairs, listening to the voice message in the elevator. It was Dani Klemperer, asking me to call him back. I checked the missed call and saw it was a different number than the gallery. His cell, probably.

I dialed and he answered on the third ring.

"Detective," he said. "Good morning."

"Same to you. You called me last night?"

"Yes, and much to my chagrin, you didn't pick up." He sighed. "Missed opportunities."

I hesitated. "Uh..."

"Oh relax, handsome. I didn't really have libertine intentions. I was just calling you back."

"Oh. Well, thanks. What did you have for me?"

"You asked if I knew where Arturo was or where he could be. The answer to the first question is no. I don't know for sure, and honestly, I don't care if I ever know where that man is at any given moment ever again. But as to where he *could* be?" He drew out the moment. "Well, I may have one possibility, if you don't already know about it. I didn't mention it before because I assumed you were aware of it. Don't the police know most everything? But then I got to thinking, what if you didn't know about it after all, and here I was assuming you did know. So when you called and asked your question in the message you left, I said to myself, 'Dani, you just call that handsome dick and tell him what you know.' And so that's what I did."

"Good news," I told Winslow as soon as I opened the door.

"Coltrane's on vacation?"

"Better than that. Dani Klemperer called me back, and guess what he told me?"

"That you could be the next Picasso?"

"No. He told me that Arturo keeps a tiny little two-room flat about two miles from A Tout le Monde. Pretty much just a bedroom and a bathroom."

"How'd we miss that?"

"He sublets it, and probably not in his name. From what I gather, he uses it for two things, depending on what kind of life situation he's in. It's either a love nest or a crash pad."

"You've got the address?"

I tapped my notepad.

"Sweet. Let's go grab the little prick."

Arturo's apartment was 3C. Dani said it was small but as we discovered so was the whole building. It had the feel of a building that had been built up in the over-sized gap between the structures on either side of it, before construction codes put a stop to that sort of thing. The super wasn't too thrilled to be woken up at eight in the morning. I resisted reminding her that eight to four were pretty much standard business hours. We didn't have a warrant for Arturo's place, and I didn't want to wait for one. So instead, we badged the super, and then made nice with her.

"Do you know the tenant in 3C?" I asked her

on the way up the narrow staircase.

"I don't really know any of the tenants," she said. "Who really knows anyone?"

"Are you familiar with him?" I tried instead.

"I might be able to pick him out of a lineup," she said, and I wasn't sure if she was joking or not. "Mostly, people pay their rent by electronic funds transfer. If they pay the rent on time, I got no reason to see them."

"What if there's a maintenance issue?"

"I take care of it, but the tenant doesn't have to be there for that. I have a key." She held up the key in her hand as proof. "It's legal for me to go inside, as long as that's the reason."

I showed her a photo of Jessica Shannon. I was curious if she'd recognize her, but I also wanted to get her off the subject of legal entry versus illegal entry. "Could you pick this one out of a lineup?" I asked. "You may have seen her with the guy from 3C."

She slowed down on the steps, then stopped and peered closer at the photo. "Maybe," she allowed. "I couldn't be sure, but I think I've seen a woman that looked something like her with the Hispanic guy. She looked a little different than in this picture, though."

"They always do," Winslow chimed in.

We got to 3C and the super slid the key into the lock. I waited until she turned the locks and cracked the door, then stepped forward and took the door by the knob. "We'll get it from here," I said. "Can you wait there?" I pointed a few feet away.

She scowled a little, showing me that she didn't approve of being excluded.

"For your safety," I added, even though I couldn't think of what danger I was protecting her from. Arturo on the other side of the door with a shotgun, I guess. Then that thought sunk in, and I hesitated long enough to draw my gun.

Winslow gave me a quizzical look, but followed suit.

I bobbed my head three times slowly and on the third time, we pushed through the door, buttonhooking onto opposite sides of the doorframe.

We didn't need to bother. Arturo didn't have a shotgun. What he did have was his belt wrapped around his neck as he hung from the back of the door that led to the bathroom. His face was discolored and his skin had a waxy look to it, even from across the room. A chair lay on its side nearby.

"Shit!" Winslow barked, and holstered his gun. He took three long strides and was at the bathroom door. He lifted Arturo's body up and reached for the belt. I moved to help him, but he stopped suddenly and stepped away.

"What is it? Why are you stopping?"

He looked over his shoulder at me. "He's cold."

That meant he'd been there since sometime last night. Hell, he might have said his farewells and kicked over the chair while Winslow and I were drinking beer in his back yard.

I heard a gasp, and looked over to see the super standing in the doorway. "Oh, no!" she stammered, all of her blasé lack of involvement falling away. "No, no, no. That's horrible."

I left Winslow's side and guided her back out into the hallway, easing the door mostly shut behind me. "What's your name, ma'am?" I asked her softly.

"Wen...Wendy," she answered. Tears brimmed her eyes.

"Wendy, I need you to do something. In a little while, some more police are going to show up outside the building. I need you to wait for them out there, and then show them up here to 3C. Can you do that, Wendy?"

She nodded woodenly. "Of course." She glanced at the apartment door. "He was young. So young."

The Last Collar

I didn't have an answer for that, so I settled for squeezing her shoulder. She turned and went downstairs. I didn't know if I could count on her to bring up the forensics people when we called them in, but it didn't matter. Mostly, I wanted to give her something to do to keep her busy and take her mind off what she'd seen.

When I went back inside 3C, Winslow was putting his phone back into his jacket pocket. "Forensics will be forty minutes—maybe an hour. They're finishing up what's probably an accidental over on Sixty-first."

I nodded, not answering. Instead, I took a look at Arturo's final work of art. He'd wrapped the buckle end of the belt around his neck and hooked the other end to...what?

It didn't take long to find the answer. I swung the door open slightly and flipped on the bathroom light. On the inside of the door was a thick hook, the kind meant for someone's bathrobe. I wouldn't have expected it to hold a body, even one of Arturo's slight frame, but upon closer inspection, I saw that it was a heavy duty hook, held in with screws, top and bottom. The door was made of thick, solid wood, and somehow that was enough to hold up the weight.

I peered at the hook. Arturo had cut a line

between two of the belt holes to create a large enough opening to fit over the hook. Even so, the belt was only just long enough to work. He must have been on his tiptoes as he stood on the chair before kicking it over.

Did he change his mind at some point? Had he suddenly had second thoughts after the chair clattered to the floor? Forensics would be able to tell me if he'd clawed at his throat to get the belt loose or if he'd meekly accepted his fate.

"Why'd he do it?" Winslow asked me from the other side of the door.

"No idea," I said in a low voice.

I went back into the living area and started scanning the room, taking mental photos. There wasn't much. A double bed with one nightstand, and a small bureau for clothing. There was a small table for two, with just one lone chair at it. A laptop computer sat there, too.

"I wonder..." I walked to the laptop. The top was up but the screen was dark.

"He's probably got a password," Winslow said. "It's probably 'Rodin' or some pretentious shit like that."

I tapped the touchpad and the screen came to life. A notepad program was the only one running, and a brief message was written there. Winslow was right about one thing. It was pretentious. At least, that was my bet.

On the laptop, Arturo had typed "I'm sorry about her" followed by "*Qualis artifex pereo!*"

Winslow appeared at my shoulder. "What the hell is that? Latin?"

"Looks like it."

"What does it say?"

"Twelve years of Catholic school, my friend. Twelve years, and you know what? I have no fucking idea." I was suddenly struck with a memory. Winslow and I were in the house and I was just about to tell him what I'd heard from Bernie Collier...

"You've got that look again, John, like you're about to shit your pants. What's up?"

"I forgot to tell you something."

"You can't be serious. Now? What the hell is it?"

"I started to tell you the other day but you cut me off."

"External attribution, John? Really?"

"Who the hell are you, Coltrane? He's throws that external attribution line around like it's going out of style, and frankly..."

"All right. Forget it. What were you supposed to tell me?"

"Jessica's doer—just before he typed 'BITCH,' he looked up something online."

"Like what?"

"He looked up the word *canicula*. It's Latin for 'bitch.'"

Chapter Thirty-Nine

"Latin, huh?" Winslow grumbled. "You couldn't remember to tell me that until now?"

"It didn't mean anything until now."

"Yeah. I guess...Jesus," he bellyached while he looked up the Latin translation on his smart phone. "Got it." Winslow boasted as if the Internet was of his creation.

"Googled it?"

"Sure did."

"Well just don't stand there—tell me what it means."

"*What an artist dies with me.*"

"Seriously?"

Winslow shrugged. "That's the way it translated but I'm still not sure what it means."

"It means Arturo was a conceited little fuck."

The flashbulb went off. "Oh. Now I get it. He's bragging." He must've had trouble reading my expression because he said, "What? What's with the puss?"

I shrugged. "You ever see a suicide note like that? I sure haven't. I'm rolling it around in my mouth and it just doesn't taste right."

Winslow grimaced. "Oh no? What does it taste like?"

"It tastes like reconstituted turkey meat covered in cheap gravy."

"Meaning?"

"It's a Swanson TV dinner, dummy. It's fast and convenient. It's food by definition but that's about all you can say about it."

Winslow gave me a cautious look. "I'm not trying to be cruel, John, but are you feeling all right?"

"Yes, I'm fine," I said hotly. "It's a metaphor. You think this guy thought long and hard about killing himself and went out with a stupid epitaph like, 'What an artist dies with me?'"

"It also says, 'I'm sorry about her.'"

"Of course it does, but—look, chime in any time now—how does it sound to you?" I turned away before Winslow could answer and examined the body. "Any chance the suicide could be staged? The Latin is a common denominator. Whoever killed Jessica killed Arturo. Don't you see?"

"You don't think he off'd himself?"

"No, I don't. Not for sure, anyway." I pulled

out my cell phone and made the call to HQ. "The autopsy will tell us for sure."

"So we gotta wait until tomorrow," Winslow griped.

"Robbery-Homicide." The voice on the other end of my phone was vaguely familiar. Then I realized it was The Ghost. "Sarge, I need the coroner at our location. You should come, too, along with the El Tee."

The Ghost cleared his throat. "Uh, sure. What do you have there?"

"Jessica Shannon's murderer," I said. "Or not."

I hung up.

Winslow gaped at me. "What the hell was that?"

I smiled. "We'll get the dog and pony show rolling, and I guarantee they'll knock out the autopsy right away. Especially with all the *high jingo* on this case."

Winslow scowled a little, but not much.

"Snap a few pictures here," I told him, stepping out of the way.

Winslow walked a slow half circle around the hanging body, using his smart phone for the photographs.

I pulled on a pair of latex gloves while I waited for him to finish with some close-ups. I pointed to his mouth. "Make sure you get a good close shot here."

"Why?

"You see a tongue protruding?"

"No."

"Exactly. Tell me how many hangings you've been to where the guy's tongue *isn't* sticking out."

He shrugged. "A few."

"Very few." I pulled over a chair. "Give me a hand here."

"With what?"

"With the body. What do you think?"

"Uh...Mocha, that's CSI's job to do. I don't want to mess up the scene. Coltrane'll skin us."

I stood up on the chair and gave Winslow a raised brow. "Detective, when coming upon a scene in which an individual appears to be in need of medical assistance, are we not duty bound to render such aid?"

He just blinked at me, then looked at Arturo. "He ain't even twitching."

"We gotta try to save him," I said. "Now come on and help me."

Winslow sighed, but put his phone away and moved forward to assist.

With glove-clad hands, I began to unhook Arturo from where his belt was hooked on the door. Winslow understood why I wanted the body down. He supported the dead man as we lowered him onto the floor. If Calderas had been strangled, I didn't want the ligature marks from the belt obliterating the ligature marks left by the strangler, not any more than had already been.

Once the body was down, I knelt next to it. "Looks like he's dead, after all," I muttered. I looked up at Winslow. "Well, we did our best."

"Just check it," Winslow said. "You're not even a little bit funny."

I loosened the belt just enough to examine the victim's neck. "See here?" I said pointing to the area near the trachea.

Winslow got down on his haunches and examined the area carefully. "Uh-huh," he concurred. "Two sets of ligature marks."

Chapter Forty

"What are you looking at?"

Winslow shook his head. "Nothing." It wasn't the truth but the truth was unimportant. On a whim it looked as if he had translated something into Latin on his smart phone.

I peered over his shoulder as we waited for coffee at the luncheonette down the block from where the artist formerly known as Arturo Calderas was cooling. The crime scene unit was tearing apart his tiny little rental, and His Majesty the Black Knight of Coltrane had ordered us to stay put until he arrived. "*A lentus ut sequi.* More Latin? What's that mean?"

"It's silly I guess but I was trying to think of something to say at..."

"My funeral?"

He wore a sad grin as he nodded. "It says, 'a tough act to follow.'"

I clipped him lightly on the chin. "You big pussy, that's so sweet. How do you translate, 'He was a God-awful pain in the ass'?"

He motioned toward the counter to where the counterman had just placed our coffee. He grabbed two hefty crumb cake squares and added them to the order.

"Don't get one for me," I said. "You know I don't eat—"

"They're for me," he blurted. "I binge eat when I'm tense."

"What are you tense about?"

"About you, you jerk."

"I'd better kick off before you weigh four-hundred pounds."

"Not funny." He quickly paid and left with his cakes and coffee.

I picked up my cup and hustled after him. "Hey, Matt, slow down." When he did I could see that he looked strained. "Hey, not now. Coltrane will be here in ten minutes and you'll let the cat out of the bag. Look..." I smiled appreciatively. "I know this stinks, but you can't let on to Coltrane about my condition. You've got to rein it in, my friend. Can you do that?"

He pulled the lid off his coffee, took a swig, and nodded unconvincingly.

"Come on. Pull it together, buddy boy. A few more days and we'll be home free and clear."

Damned if it didn't look as if he was going to cry. "I love you, Matt, and I'm deeply touched. We've been partners a long time, but please...you've got to tough it out a little longer, okay?" He nodded again, no more convincing than his first attempt.

"Look, there's a FedEx across the street and I've got to get that check on its way to Sandra. I'll be right back. If Coltrane gets here before I'm back, tell him I had to see a man about a horse or whatever you feel like telling him. I really don't care."

Winslow exhaled a big humid sigh and unwrapped the first of his crumb cakes. "Aw'right. Meet you there."

I grabbed my coffee and bolted across the street.

I couldn't believe my eyes—I was pretty sure that I saw Coltrane doing a happy dance and high-fiving Winslow at the crime scene. I checked my pulse to make sure I hadn't passed to the other side. Could that be what heaven is like for cops, one big crime scene where all the leads pan out, none of the perps get away, and the brass is always happy? I could live with that, but it was more likely though that Coltrane would brandish a fiery pitchfork and chase me through gobs of crackhead spew for eternity. I'd be stupid not to set a reasonable level of expectation for myself.

His expression turned cooler as I approached. "Winslow tells me this may be Jessica Shannon's killer."

"The jury is still out."

His expression said, *fuck me*. "He also tells me you don't like this as a suicide."

"Yeah. That's right. I'm suspicious, at least."

"Why?"

"Did you read the suicide note?"

"*Yeah?*"

"No way he wrote that crock of shit. I'll bet we find a second set of prints on that computer keyboard. Did Winslow tell you about the Latin, and how—"

"That don't mean shit." He turned toward the corpse. "Nothing says numb nuts didn't Google the Latin himself."

"I don't see it."

He smacked Winslow's shoulder. He probably meant it playfully but it made Winslow wince. "Look at that, Mocha's a clairvoyant. I'm going to start calling him the Perp Whisperer. Ha!"

"I'm glad you're laughing about all this but there are definitely two sets of ligature marks on the vic's neck."

"Maybe," he grumbled. "So all of a sudden you're a coroner?"

"I'm a detective."

"All right, then, *Detective*, talk to me and tell me why I shouldn't consider the case closed."

I took a deep breath and plunged in.

Chapter Forty-One

"Let's talk about the people evidence first," I told Coltrane.

"By all means."

"There's no way Arturo would kill himself."

Coltrane raised his brows. "It looks like he just did."

"Look like it, yeah, but I have serious doubts. Arturo was a narcissist to the nth degree. He thought he was a great artist—"

"Yeah, I saw the note," Coltrane said. "Pretty lofty shit, comparing yourself to a Roman emperor."

Winslow and I just stared at him.

Coltrane stared back. "You didn't recognize the quote?"

We both shook our heads.

Coltrane nodded toward me. "Didn't you go to Catholic school? What'd they teach you there?"

"That beating off was going to make me go blind. What's this about a Roman?"

Coltrane sighed. "That Latin phrase? Those were Nero's dying words. You know, the Roman emperor?"

"He the one that fiddled while the city burned?" Winslow asked.

"That's the rumor," Coltrane said.

I tapped my chin and thought some more. Then I said, "Well, that only strengthens my theory."

"How's that?"

"First, let's be clear on Arturo. He was a manipulative prick, and a total narcissist. It would be way out of character for him to kill himself."

"How about to kill someone else? As in, Jessica Shannon?"

I thought about that. "I could see him doing that," I admitted. "Pretty easily, in fact. Hell, that's the reason we came here."

"But you finding him swinging from his own belt, and suddenly he's not your number one suspect anymore?" Coltrane gave me a hard look. "If I didn't know better, I'd think you were just trying to make this as difficult as possible, Mocha. Just because."

"I'm not," I assured him. "I want to close this case. I just want to close it right, that's all."

He eyed me for a moment, then motioned me to continue.

"A type-written note," I said. "Pretty convenient. No need to match hand-writing."

"It's the new millennium," Coltrane replied. "Has been for a long time. Everything's digital now. Hell, people leave suicide notes on social media now."

"Fine," I allowed. "But that quote? Now way Arturo wrote that. It's way too pretentious for a guy like him."

"Pretentious?" Coltrane said. "He was an artist."

"True, but he came from the streets. He hustled, he schemed, he scammed. He wasn't the kind of guy who learned history or Latin phrases."

"He ran in those circles, didn't he? Maybe he got interested once he was part of the elite."

"I don't think so. Too much work, and he would have been spending all of his time working on whatever con he was working." I shrugged. "And, to be fair, it looks like he spent a lot of time working on his sculptures, too. But I don't think he picked up Latin or history in his spare time. No. Someone else wrote that phrase to try to capture Arturo's persona, but him writing it is a miss."

Coltrane just stared at me, not conceding the point, but listening.

"So from a people perspective, it's unlikely that

Arturo would kill himself or that he would leave this note. And when you look at the physical evidence, it looks unlikely there, too. In fact, it looks like someone strangled him, and then hung him to fake a suicide."

Coltrane digested what I said, then he asked, "What physical evidence?"

"His tongue wasn't sticking out of his mouth, for one, and it should be. That's a sure sign of death by hanging."

Coltrane gave me a dubious look. "One that happens every time?"

"No," I admitted. "But most of the time."

"But not all the time."

"No."

"So you got nothing definitive, then," Coltrane said.

"We've got two sets of ligature marks," I said. "One from strangulation, and one from the hanging. The hanging marks will show as post-mortem."

"What if he tried to hang himself twice?" Coltrane asked. "Maybe he just fucked up the first go round."

I shrugged. "I'm not saying that couldn't happen, but there's no evidence to support it."

"There's no evidence to support your theory,

either," Coltrane said. "For all we know, Jessica Shannon's killer got a case of the remorses, or figured the jig was up and he didn't want to go to prison. Either way, he offed himself, even if it was a little sloppy."

"Push the autopsy through immediately," I urged him. "Dollars to donuts, they'll find a broken hyoid bone in the throat."

Coltrane peered at me cautiously. "A broken what? You want to speak English?"

"The hyoid bone." I pointed to my own throat. "It's here. And if it's broken, then Arturo was more likely strangled, and not a hanging suicide."

Coltrane flicked his eyes to Winslow. "That true?"

Winslow nodded. "Sure is, El Tee."

"Even if it isn't broken," I continued, "that doesn't mean he wasn't strangled. It only breaks about half the time in strangulation cases, but it'll be broken in this one."

"Why do you say that?"

I looked over at Winslow, then back at Coltrane. "Because whoever did this is the same person who killed Jessica Shannon, and he has strong hands."

Coltrane stroked his chin. "This artist guy..."

"Arturo."

"Right, Arturo. He was a sculptor, right?"

"Yes."

"So he had strong hands, right?"

"Yes."

"And up until an hour ago, you liked him for the Shannon murder?"

"Yes," I admitted. "I did."

"But not now?"

"No," I said confidently. "I don't."

Coltrane turned to Winslow. "You agree with this?"

Winslow nodded slowly. "Yes, sir. I do."

"Here's the thing," I told Coltrane. "He was a good suspect. If he'd been alive when we got to the apartment, I would have arrested him. But he wasn't. He was dead. Only he didn't kill himself. Someone did it, and staged this suicide. Why?"

"You're the detective," Coltrane groused.

"It's simple," I said. "They did it because we're getting too close. Like I said, whoever killed Arturo, killed Jessica Shannon."

Coltrane looked at me hard for a long while. Finally, he let out a long sigh. "Fine, Mocha. I'll push the autopsy to the front of the line, and we'll see if they get any prints off the keyboard. But if the prints come up empty or this dude's hi-ho bone isn't broken, we're calling this one solved. You get me?"

I didn't protest. It wouldn't have done any good. All I could do now was hope I was right. Besides, I had a bigger problem to worry about. If I was right and Arturo wasn't Jessica Shannon's killer, then I still had to figure out who was.

Chapter Forty-Two

I figured I had enough airline credit card points for a trip to Saturn and back, but with the late booking penalty and all the shitty economy cutbacks I had to empty my bonus points account for a one-way first class flight to San Diego. I suppose I'd have been really pissed off if I was planning to do a lot of traveling in the future but where I was headed after San Diego...well, you didn't need jet engines to get you there.

I didn't believe in bank vaults and truthfully, I didn't have anything worth locking up. I wasn't even sure if I needed a will. All I had to do was add Sandra and Sophia to my Chase savings account. As bad as my relationship with Sandra was, I had no doubt that she'd only spend my savings the right way, and my department death benefits...well, that was already a done deal. Sophia had been added to the official paperwork practically the day she was born.

Doc Stiviak had told me not to take more than

two Relpax tablets in one day but like a lot of the other advice he'd given me, I ignored it. He'd told me to avoid triggers like stress, excessive amounts of caffeine, and alcohol, points I considered moot. So I dropped another tab to keep the pain from crushing my skull.

How can a cop avoid stress? My career was dwindling down to scant days and then would come the hard part, reconciling with Sandra and my little girl. Dying was the easy part, easy on me anyway. Hospice, a morphine pump, my immediate family, and a chaplain—they had the hard part. All I had to do was close my eyes and go to sleep.

I was thinking about my folks. I'd already dropped the bomb, but telling them I was going to San Diego to die, knowing we'd never see each other again. I couldn't imagine the news not killing them as well.

I had an unopened bottle of Johnnie Walker Blue Label in the pantry and well, hell, I wasn't leaving the planet without it. It had been a birthday gift from the boys on the squad and I was saving it for a special occasion. I cracked the seal and poured two fingers into my favorite drinking glass—smacked my lips after the first mouthful of liquid fire had glided down my throat. My bucket list was a short one: solve the Shannon homicide, hug my little girl, and wipe out my bottle of primo scotch whiskey. My priorities had been clearly established.

Six fingers of scotch and my brain-pain pills did the trick. I went out like a light. It was six a.m. when Coltrane woke me. "That fucking hyoid piece of shit was crushed," he grumbled.

"I told you it would be."

"Yeah, well the doc also said that it only breaks in about twenty-five percent of hangings, too, so I think we're safe sticking with this as a suicide."

"Did he mention which twenty-five?" I asked.

"Huh?"

"Did he mention how that twenty-five percent is almost exclusively old people with brittle bones? Not young males in the prime of health?"

Coltrane sighed. "I want this to be finished, Mocha."

"So do I."

He was quiet a minute. Then he said, "Get back to work."

Chapter Forty-Three

There were no other prints on the keyboard other than Arturo's, but I half-expected that to be the case. It didn't take a genius—wear gloves, or...I tell you there's nothing like a bottle of two hundred-dollar hooch to grease the wheels. Arturo's prints were on the keyboard so it hadn't been wiped down. That meant the perp wore gloves or...I had a sudden vision of Eva's fingernails clicking away on the keyboard. Christ, I could hear them in my head. French tips actually, long polished fingernails with white tips. She wasn't the only one, either. A former squad admin, a Boricua who wore tight jeans over her ample ass and the same red patent leather pumps every day used to clatter away with claws like that, too, and I remembered that the noise drove me up the wall.

"Matt?" I looked across the squad but Winslow was not at his desk. I jumped up and scoured the building. I caught up with Winslow as he was coming out of the men's room. His hands were still damp as he adjusted his waistband and holster. "Grab your jacket, slick. I've got a hunch."

"We'd like to see Wendy," Winslow said as soon as the door opened.

The man standing in front of us was stout with a mustache and an obvious comb-over. He had a thick accent and an obstinate disposition. "What?" he asked unhappily. From the noise blaring from the TV set it sounded as if we'd pulled him away from the ball game.

Back to square one. I pulled my gold shield. "We're city homicide detectives."

"And I'm missing the game of the year. Come back later. Wendy's not home."

Motherfucker. Never piss off a cop on his way to the hereafter. I stepped past him into the apartment.

"Where the hell are you going?" he shouted.

I found the remote and shut off the TV.

He followed me into the apartment. "Are you crazy?"

"It's baseball—nothing's going to change in the next five minutes."

"Christ!"

"What's your name?"

"Victor."

"Well, Victor, you heard that a body was found here yesterday, no?"

He corrected me, "Suicide. The male prostitute? You think I'm surprised? The man sucked cock for a living—he probably had AIDS."

"I didn't ask if you were surprised. The victim may not have committed suicide."

"Someone killed him?"

"We're still investigating," Winslow said. He pulled a photo out of his pocket. "Take a look at this."

Victor took the photo from Winslow and studied it. "Oh this one. I remember her. She's got a great ass, like a linebacker she's built. I'd like to hit that rear end and drive it over the end zone."

It sounded like Victor was a devotee of doggie style. Wendy was a lucky girl; she didn't have to look at his face when he nailed her. "Did she come around a lot?"

He shrugged. "Used to. It's been a while, though."

"How about yesterday? You see her here yesterday?"

"No. I was in Atlantic City for the day. The Borgota runs a shuttle bus from the supermarket parking lot."

"How'd you do?" Winslow asked.

"Big winner. Big, big winner," he boasted. "I own the craps table."

"So you didn't see the linebacker yesterday."

"No. The bus left at seven in the morning."

"When's Wendy coming back?" Winslow asked.

"Monday."

"Monday?" I blurted. *Shit! I'll be three thousand miles west of here by then.*

"Yeah. All the police activity shook her up. She's spending the weekend with her parents."

"And where's that?" Winslow asked.

"Florida. She left out of MacArthur Airport this morning."

Chapter Forty-Four

I had trouble thinking with my eyes closed, but a blinding headache left me little choice as we rode back toward Lenny's place to take one last crack at him. With my eyes open, the sun burned into my head. It was as if God was pointing a death ray straight at me.

My confederate, Winslow, was behind the wheel. "What made you think of the sister, Morgan?"

I shrugged. "Long fingernails on the keyboard," I said. "And all that Latin jazz. Her father being a stuffed shirt attorney, he probably dropped Latin pearls all over the house. *E pluribus unum*, and all that pompous drivel."

"Huh?"

"It doesn't matter. She was right there in front of us the whole time. We were stupid not to consider her."

"I don't know about *stupid*," Winslow said.

I raised my hand and ticked off the reasons.

"She found the body, but we looked right past her as a suspect. Then the bit with dating Lenny and then Arturo? That reeks of sibling rivalry, and remember she told us in that first interview that Jessica was her parent's favorite?"

"Yeah," Winslow admitted with a sigh. "I remember."

"She's the one that steered us to Arturo and to Lenny, too."

"Still," Winslow said, "we were looking for someone strong enough to strangle someone from behind. A juice head and a sculptor are pretty good suspects."

"True enough. But so is a rock climber."

He thought about that, recalling our interview with Morgan. "Shit, how could I have let that slip between the cracks?"

"It was a mistake, but that's done now. The important thing is that we're onto her now."

"So Victor recognized Morgan from the photo? That's good."

"Good *and* bad," I responded still squeezing my eyes shut. "Good if Wendy saw her coming or going from Arturo's apartment yesterday. Real bad if she didn't." A smart defense attorney would argue that Morgan had been a frequent visitor, creating a plausible explanation for finding her prints in the apartment, if we were lucky enough to find them.

I'd wired Morgan's photo to the Dade County Sheriff's office. A deputy was going to track down Wendy to ask if she recognized Morgan and if she'd seen her yesterday. That would be enough to pick her up.

"So why are we going to Lenny's now?" Winslow asked. "Why not just grab her first?"

"I want to ask him more about Morgan, and he might have known about the Arturo affair, too."

"That's all circumstantial."

"True. But circumstantial evidence is still evidence."

Winslow scratched the whiskers on his cheek. "So here's the problem I've got. Say she is the doer. How do you figure she managed to hoist one hundred and fifty pounds of dead weight?"

"With great difficulty." I winced as a terrible ache darted across my cerebrum.

"Hey, you all right?" Winslow asked. "I think I've got Aleve."

He wanted to be helpful but had no idea how much pain I was in. Trying to kill my headache with a couple of Aleve tabs was like trying to extinguish a volcano with a squirt gun. "Thanks, but I took something before I left the house this morning."

"That's the tumor?" he hesitantly asked.

"Yup. Coming on like gangbusters."

"Why don't I drop you off home? I can do the interviews on my own. You can lie down, maybe put a cool washcloth on your forehead—usually works for me."

"This is the way it's going to be, Matt. I already doubled up on my meds. Just have to grin and bear it."

"Really? Nothing will help?"

"Nothing much." I pointed across the avenue. "There's a spot, pull up in front of Starbucks. Sometimes a cold caffeinated drink helps."

"I'll grab them." Winslow turned the AC up to max and aimed the vents at my head. "Be right back. Maybe we can freeze it out."

"Maybe. Thanks."

He wasn't gone two minutes when my cell buzzed. I opened my eyes just enough to read the display and see that Dr. Stiviak was calling, no doubt to see if I had honored our deal. "Five p.m. tomorrow, Doc," I told him without saying hello. "I'll punch out for good."

"You've informed your supervisor then?"

Lie like a rug. What the hell can he do to you anyway? "I booked a one-way flight to

California—leaving this weekend." There. I hadn't lied so much as avoided his question.

He answered with the utmost sincerity, "Good. I think it's for the best, John. Like we talked about."

"That's right, just like we talked about. Splurged as a matter of fact—I'm flying first class. Do you think they have prettier flight attendants in first class?"

He answered facetiously, "Yes. Of course they do. But I really called to see how you were feeling. How's the pain?"

"It feels like the Jets are running over my face."

"Double up your dosage," he offered immediately.

"Yeah. Well. Uh. Dr. Moccia tried that already."

"No relief?"

"A couple of hours and then wham, it came back like a sledgehammer."

The doctor was momentarily silent. "I can write you a prescription for morphine, John. There's no reason for you to suffer. The tumor must be growing rapidly. You may want to arrange for hospice care as soon as you get to California."

"That's all right, Doctor. Let's put the narcotics and adult diapers on hold for now."

"It's up to you, John, but don't put too much pressure on yourself. No one is judging you."

I am. Winslow was on his way back to the car. "Thanks for the call, Doctor. I'll be in touch if I need anything else."

Winslow got in and handed me the clear plastic cup. I took a long hard pull on the straw and sucked down a mouthful iced cold Starbucks rocket fuel. "Ah, that's refreshing. Know what I could really go for now?"

"Pastry?"

"Nah. A world class blowjob."

He grimaced. "If you think it'll help."

"Relax, Junior." I teased him by running my fingers through his hair. "You look like a gagger anyway."

Chapter Forty-Five

We knocked at Lenny's door, but there was no answer. So we did what cops always do. We knocked again, harder.

Still no answer.

"You figure he flew the coop?" Winslow asked.

I shook my head. "Why would he? He didn't try to avoid us before."

Winslow sighed. "Yeah, but it wouldn't be the first time someone cooperated and then turned out to be involved." He held his hands. "As in, your theory with the sister."

"You're right," I admitted. "And we know she and Lenny were lovers. But..."

"What?"

"I just don't see it," I said. "I think he was being honest about being over both of the Shannon women. I think he really was moving on."

"Rehabilitated, huh?" Winslow sounded dubious.

"It's gotta work some of the time," I said.

"Broken clock's right twice a day, too."

I ignored him and knocked one last time. We waited and listened.

No answer.

"You never answered my question, Sherlock," Winslow said.

"What question?"

"Morgan. How the hell did she lift Arturo up to hang him there?"

I nodded. "Yeah, that's a problem, huh?"

"Sorta blows your theory to shit, actually."

Pain pulsed in my temple. I leaned against the wall with one hand and bowed my head.

"You okay?"

"Sure," I said. "I'm great."

"Mocha, maybe we oughta—"

"You wanna know how she did it?" I interrupted. "I'll tell you. She strangled him with her hands, first off. Just like she did to her sister."

"Takes strong hands to do that."

"Which a rock climber would have."

"Say that's true. Still, what's she weigh?"

I considered. "A buck thirty?"

Winslow made a *maybe* expression. "I'll give you that, if she's got some lean muscle on her. Still, lifting a hundred and fifty pounds is a lot."

"I don't know if Arturo weighed that much. He

could have been closer to one-thirty himself."

"Now you're just trying to fudge things to fit your theory."

"No," I said. "You wait. I'll bet the autopsy report has him closer to one-thirty than one-fifty."

"Sure, with all the blood out of him."

I sighed. "All right. Let's go with one-fifty, but you gotta agree that she's a strong woman, right?"

He shrugged. "She was in good shape, and if she had the hand strength to strangle Jessica from behind...yeah, all right."

"So, she used that strength to strangle him and then hang him from the door with his own belt. Then she typed the message and—"

He held up his hand. "Wait. You're assuming she's strong enough to do that."

"I am."

"That's a big assumption."

"You don't think Morgan did it?"

His eyes told me everything.

"Son of a *bitch*. You think Arturo killed Jessica and then offed himself? Out of what, guilt?"

"I don't know, man. That's just it. I mean, the two ligatures marks could mean he was killed, but it could mean he was just a fuck up and it took him two go rounds to manage to kill himself."

"The hyoid bone was fractured," I argued.

"That's a clear sign of strangulation."

"Yeah, but that happens sometimes in hangings, too."

"Not as often, and mostly in old people."

"I know. But not always. And..."

"And what?"

He shrugged. "I'm just thinking about Austin's razor."

"Huh?"

"Austin's razor. You told me about it once. That the simplest answer is the most likely?"

"*Occam's* razor," I corrected. "Not Austin's."

"It doesn't matter. I got the idea right, didn't I?"

He had, but I wasn't letting go that easily. "I could maybe buy Arturo as the doer, Matt, but I definitely don't buy his suicide, or that note. And if someone killed him, and faked the suicide, then Arturo is *not* our guy."

"But you like Morgan for it instead."

"I do."

"Even with the fact there's no way she was strong enough?"

"Maybe she had help."

"Oh, now she had help? The worm turns."

"Sometimes the answer *isn't* the most obvious one," I said.

"I'm just worried, partner."

"About what?"

"That because of your condition and everything, you want this to go a certain way. That maybe that and the tumor are affecting your thinking."

I didn't have a reply for him.

We stood silently in the hallway, grinding on that. I think we both realized we were still outside of Lenny's door at about the same time. I gave it one more hard rap for good measure, but we really didn't wait for an answer. Instead, we turned and headed back to the car.

As I reached for the passenger door handle, my phone buzzed. I steeled myself for Coltrane's bellows, Sandra's bitching, or maybe even Stiviak following up, but what I saw was "Gastineau."

"Who is it?" Winslow asked.

"The Ghost." I punched the button. "Moccia."

"I'm getting tired of relaying your messages, Detective," the Ghost said without preamble. "Why don't you set up call forwarding from your desk like the rest of the human race?"

"I'll do that first thing Monday," I told him, and that actually made me smile. I caught Winslow grinning, too. "What's the message?"

"Dade County got in touch with your wit down there. Wendy something or other?"

"And?"

"She positively identified the woman in the picture as having frequented the artist's crash pad a while back."

"When was the last time she saw her there?"

"Yesterday."

A thrill went through me. I loved that moment, when all your hunches and theories all come together under one roof, and the case is busted open. My smile broadened. "That's the best news I've had all week, Sarge."

"Yeah, well, good. You can tell it to Coltrane."

"Can you handle that? You're already at the station, right? We're going to head over and pick up our suspect."

"No, I can't."

"Why not?"

"I'm going home sick," Gastineau said, and hung up.

Good to know some things will never change, even after I'm gone.

Winslow was watching me as I broke the connection. His eyes were lit up. "So you were right, then?"

"Yep. Wendy ID'd Morgan and put her there yesterday. We'll have to get a detailed statement from her, but..."

Winslow beamed at me. "Damn, son. Why did I ever doubt you?"

"Because you're retarded."

He smiled right through the insult. "I love you, man."

"The feeling's mutual, Corky. Now, let's go pick up a murderer."

Chapter Forty-Six

The housekeeper let us in at the Shannon residence without a word. When we asked to speak to Morgan, she led us through the house, up a long sweeping set of stairs and to a massive veranda, complete with a pool and a wet bar.

These people sure knew how to live.

Morgan Shannon was lying on a beach recliner. She wore a skimpy bathing suit and her hair was up. I couldn't tell if she was watching us approach or not because of the sunglasses on her face, but her relaxed pose never changed.

Once we were close enough to talk, the housekeeper left us, disappearing into the house again. Winslow and I moved a little closer to her, flanking both sides of the chair casually.

"Miss Shannon?" I said. "We need to talk."

She raised a hand and slid the glasses down her nose to look at me. "Detective...Nokia, was it?"

"Moccia," I said. "And Winslow. We're working your sister's murder."

She nodded, and sat up. I noticed that she didn't have the exaggerated muscle definition of a body builder, but her body was toned and supple, and she moved with athletic grace. Or maybe Winslow was right, and I saw that because I wanted to.

"What can I do for you?" she asked me, her voice smooth. "I think I answered all of your questions before, didn't I?"

"We have some more questions."

"Is it about Lenny? Was he the one?"

"You mean the Lenny you had an affair with?" I asked quietly. "That Lenny?"

Her face froze for a moment, but then she brushed my words away. "What does *that* matter? He was a charming, manipulative man. I was vulnerable. So what?"

"So what," I agreed. "Do you want to put some clothes on, Miss Shannon?"

"Whatever for?"

"The trip down to the police station."

"That's not necessary. I can answer your questions right here. How many do you have, after all?"

"Oh, a few," I said. "Why don't you throw something on and we'll finish this conversation at the precinct?"

"I don't understand."

"Well, let's see if you understand this. You have the right to remain silent. Anything you say can and will be used—"

"This is ludicrous."

"—against you in a court of law. You have the right to an attorney, and to have that attorney present during questioning, if you so desire. If you cannot afford an attorney—"

"My father *is* an attorney!" she snapped.

I smiled humorlessly. "If you cannot afford an attorney, one will be provided to you without cost by the court. Now, do you understand these rights, Miss Shannon?"

"Of course I do. I'm not stupid."

"You want to waive these rights and answer my questions?"

"I already told you I'd answer your questions, but if you're going to—"

"Okay," I interrupted. "How about this question: why did you date Lenny?"

She hesitated, biting her lip. Then she said, "I already explained that. He was charming, and good at manipulation."

"So he pursued you?"

"Yes, of course."

"Even from prison?"

She swallowed, then moved to toss her hair

back. The move didn't work, since her hair was already up and bound close to her head, but she didn't seem to notice. "I just didn't want to abandon him," she said. "Prison seems like such a horrible place, and he had no one. So I tried to be a friend to him."

I nodded like I understood. Then I asked, "How about Arturo?"

"What about him?"

"Why date him? Another of your sister's exes?"

She didn't act surprised, and shrugged. "It just worked out that way. We ran into each other occasionally, so yeah, it became a thing. So what? Are you trying to find my sister's killer or protect my chastity?"

"Why didn't you tell us about your relationship with Arturo?"

"Because it was none of your business."

"You didn't think it was relevant?"

"It wasn't. Same with Lenny. If one of them had something to do with Jessica's death, it doesn't involve me. And if neither of them had anything to do with it, then my relationship with either one isn't relevant. Either way, who I fuck is none of your business."

"True enough," I said. "So when did you stop fucking Arturo?"

"None of your business."

"How about Jessica? When did she stop?" My investigation, including Arturo's statement, pointed to months ago, but I was curious what Morgan would say.

She didn't answer right away, and slid the glasses back up to cover her eyes. Finally, she said, "I...I saw them together a couple of weeks ago at a bar. One of those places all the artsy people hang out. They were at the bar, laughing. It looked like they were...together again. That's what made me think Arturo was the one that hurt her. That maybe she rejected him, and he couldn't handle it, or something like that." She tilted her head toward me. "I tried to point you in that direction, to help you out. What's the problem? Can't you find him?"

I shook my head. "We found him."

"Well, then, there you have it. If you even manage a half-ass job, you'll get him to confess and this whole mess will be solved."

I leaned forward and lowered my voice. "Arturo's dead, Morgan. We found him hanging in his little apartment."

She stared at me for a long moment, then her lip quivered. She dropped her face into her hand and sniffled.

I played along, putting my hand on her shoulder. "I'm sorry for your loss," I murmured.

"I can't believe he's dead," she said, half sobbing. "But if he killed Jessica, then he deserved it."

"He didn't kill her," I said in the same soothing tones.

I felt her tense slightly, but only slightly. I decided the time had come.

"Morgan, maybe you can tell me what you were doing at Arturo's place yesterday morning?"

This time, her entire body stiffened, and her sniffling stopped mid-sob.

"What the *hell* is going on here?" a voice bellowed.

I turned to see Martin Shannon standing a few feet away, his face contorted in anger.

And then all hell broke loose.

Chapter Forty-Seven

An outraged Martin Shannon moved forward. "Honey, what's going on? What are you doing?"

"They think I killed Jessica, Daddy. And Arturo."

He turned his gaze to me. "Is that true, Detective?"

I nodded. "It is. If you want to get her an attorney, I'd advise doing it now."

He pointed. "There's no way she killed her sister. That's ridiculous."

No? What about Arturo, pops? I thought. What I said was, "Then she should come down to station and explain, and we'll work everything out."

Shannon seemed to consider my words, then turned to his daughter. "Honey, he's right. Go with them. I'll call my attorney, and we'll get this straightened out. All of it."

"No," Morgan said simply.

Shannon held up his hands. "No? Don't be silly. You're a Shannon. We can handle this, like I said.

All of it."

"Handle what?" I asked.

They both froze for a moment. Shannon's eyes darted between us before returning to Morgan. Small beads of sweat popped out on his upper lip. He wiped them away.

Morgan sighed and sank into the pool recliner. "Oh, God," she said heavily. "I can't do this anymore."

Shannon held up his hands. "Honey, don't say another word. Just wait for my lawyer."

Morgan's voice was small, but loud enough for Winslow and me to hear every word. "He did it. He choked Arturo, and hung him. He thought Arturo was the murderer, so he went there and he—"

"Don't lie!" Shannon snapped.

"Lies are all I know," Morgan replied in a flat tone.

Shannon's gaze did another lap between Winslow and me before settling on his daughter again. His tone softened. "Fine, no lies. I'll tell them what happened. You didn't do anything wrong. He was attacking you, just like he attacked Jessica. It was self-defense, and..."

"And then after I killed him, I called you, and you came and cleaned up my mess. Is that what you were going to say, Daddy?"

Shannon shot me a sidelong glance. "You're upset. Just let me do the talking, baby girl."

"Don't call me that."

"It's going to be okay."

"No," Morgan said heavily. "It's not. It never will be okay."

We fell silent, watching Shannon stare nervously at his daughter. Neither Winslow nor I were going to interrupt this exchange. It was a veritable gold mine.

"You loved her more," Morgan finally said, her tone strangled with pain. "No matter what I did, you loved her more. Even after she was gone, you still love her more."

Martin Shannon said nothing.

"I tried everything," Morgan continued in a thick voice. I glanced down at her to see tears streaming down her face. "I was first, Daddy. *Me*, not her. And I gave you...everything, but you still loved her more."

"Don't say anything else," Shannon urged. "Just stop talking, and we'll get through this. Don't say another word."

"Don't say another word about what?" Morgan snapped back, an edge creeping back into her voice. "Which secrets are you worried about,

Daddy? What I did to Jessica, or what you did to me?"

Shannon didn't miss a beat. He held out his arms. "Come on, now, baby girl."

Morgan's face softened momentarily.

"That's it," Shannon said soothingly. "Everything is going to be all right."

Morgan stared at him, her expression full of longing and heartbreak.

"Come to Daddy, baby girl," Shannon murmured.

She shook her head, her expression turning hopeless. "Never again," she whispered. Then she looked up at me. "I'm so tired. So, so tired."

"I know," I said quietly.

"Stay the hell out of this," Shannon spat. "This is none of your—"

Winslow rose to his full, intimidating height and squared off with the old shit. "This is none of our what?" he snapped. His callous expression shut Shannon down cold.

I approached Morgan and kneeled so that I was eye to eye with her on the pool recliner and took her hands in mine. "I think there was something you wanted to say," I said in an encouraging tone.

She nodded as tears rushed forth.

And then she told me everything.

Chapter Forty-Eight

The first thing that was hard to do was to hear her confession. It was ugly, tired, and resigned, but without remorse.

The second thing that was hard to do was to restrain Martin Shannon.

First we had to stop him from going after his daughter. Then we had to fight to get the handcuffs on. For an older man who grew up with a silver spoon, he was a handful. He even knocked Winslow into the pool before I was able to get behind him, snake my arms around his neck, and put him to sleep long enough to cuff him.

Winslow crawled out of the pool and stood next to me, water streaming off of his clothing and onto the warm concrete. Morgan sat still on the pool recliner, watching the whole scene dispassionately.

After about thirty seconds of both of us breathing hard and trying to catch our breath, Detective Matt Winslow summed it all up perfectly.

The Last Collar

"Ho-ly *shit*," he wheezed.
"Amen, brother."

Chapter Forty-Nine

I had to run it for Coltrane a second time before he was clear on things.

"The goddamn sister, huh? Why?"

I shrugged. "That's one for the psychologists to figure out, but sibling envy isn't exactly a new concept, El Tee. Daddy obviously favored the younger daughter. I'm bet-ting that Morgan was trying to one up her sister by taking on or even stealing her men. So when she saw Jessica and Arturo together at a bar recently..." I snapped my fingers. "She'd had enough."

"So they were fighting over that slimy little sculptor the whole time?"

I shook my head. "I don't think so. There's no evidence of it. In fact, if I had to guess, I'd say that Jessica and Arturo simply had a chance meeting, just like Arturo said."

"And coincidentally, the sister spotted them?"

"Not the biggest of coincidences, if she still had the hots for Arturo. She'd go to his hangouts, wouldn't she?"

"How the hell would I know?" he asked with resentment creeping into his voice. "You for sure put Martin Shannon in handcuffs."

So that's why he's pissed. "He's a collar," I said. "Aiding and abetting after the fact, for starters. He helped her set up the suicide scene at Arturo's."

There was something else, too. The way he'd called to her—*Come to Daddy, baby girl*—and the way she'd whispered before turning to me and spilling all of her dark secrets. Or most of them.

Never again.

I couldn't prove it, but it was pretty obvious what had gone on inside the Shannon residence all these years. It was a dark place, at least for Morgan, and one I'm sure would come out as the case moved through the court system.

Coltrane nodded. "I understand his actions are criminal, but no jury is ever going to convict him. I mean, think about it. He believed the guy who murdered one of his daughters tried to do the same to his other daughter, too, but instead she killed him in self-defense. Then she called him? What he did, he was only trying to protect her."

Come to Daddy, baby girl.

Yeah, Martin Shannon was *such* a great guy. "By illegally altering a crime scene and staging a suicide. He's a collar, El Tee."

"Goddamnit, I *know* he's a collar. All right? But it's not going to hold up, and you know who his lawyer is? Prepare yourself, because they're going to tear you up like an old tennis shoe at trial."

I was quiet a minute. Then I said, "Actually, I think Winslow will be the one that gets that honor."

"Huh?"

"I need to tell you something, Lieutenant. And then..." I took a deep breath and let it out. "And then, I think I'm going to be done with the job."

Chapter Fifty

Winslow showed up right on time, early actually, and he was driving his baby blue '64 Mustang convertible, the one he'd start restoring the same day he put in his papers. He'd talked about it for years, planned for years, and was now finally on the cusp of executing his dream. The car had some rust and rattled like a bag full of wrenches, but the top was down and the sun was out. The blast of fresh air in my face helped me forget that I was coming close to clocking out for good.

He was smiling ear to ear as he piloted the vintage pony car along the Grand Central Parkway. It was late afternoon and there was conspicuously little traffic on the notoriously congested roadway.

"You were right even before you knew you were right," Winslow said with a wide grin on his face.

"Meaning?"

"I got a call from the crime lab before I left to pick you up. Morgan's fingerprints were all over the cash we found in Arturo's storage locker."

"Son of a bitch! You think he knew she killed her sister from the very beginning?"

"Looks that way."

I grunted in admiration. "He never let on about it, not once."

"Maybe, but nothing says guilty like a bagful of extortion money. I'm surprised he hung around after collecting the payoff."

"Maybe he asked for more. Maybe he told her the police were busting his ass and he was gonna spill unless she anted up again."

"Maybe."

"Yeah. Maybe." I tilted my head back and let the sun warm my face. "Even if he didn't ask for more cash, just the idea that he was our number one suspect was sufficient motivation for her to ice him. I called her to say that we were looking for him. I left her a message. Remember? She must've figured we were about to squeeze him like a loofa sponge and that she was about to get fingered for the deed."

"Unless her lawyer gets her to retract her confession, she'll talk to me in follow-up interviews. We'll eventually know for certain."

"Either way, Daddy Fuckface goes to jail, too."

Winslow smiled evilly. "I have to tell you—the

idea of nailing her old man delights me even more than nailing her. What a nasty old prick. Twist of fate don't you think? The high and mighty attorney in a maximum security facility brushing his teeth daily with inmate cock."

I snickered. "I love it when you're cruel. Solves the Big Bang Theory about Morgan's ability to stage the hanging for us, anyway."

He chuckled. "You know, the more I think about Daddy Shannon getting butt raped, the more it's making me smile on the inside."

Winslow's comment made me cackle. "Why, you Machiavellian son of a bitch. I had no idea you harbored all that venom." I slapped him on the shoulder. "Good for you."

"Crap!" Our light traffic serendipity was short-lived. The Grand Central slowed to a crawl as we approached the entrance to the Van Wyck. Winslow looked none too happy. "Poor Morgan Shannon, all that money and the self-esteem of a redheaded step child."

We were now at a complete standstill. I tilted my head and shot Winslow an expression that said, "Come on, man, don't you get it?"

"What?" he asked seeing that I was disappointed.

"That's exactly what she was. That comment

about what he did to her? 'Come to Daddy, baby girl?' The look in her eyes when the old prick said that. Her abject refusal, 'Never again?'"

I waited for Winslow to figure it out.

His nose wrinkled in disgust. "So he was doing his own daughter, the miserable old shit?"

"I believe he was. Everything Morgan did, she did to earn recognition from the old man. Jessica was obviously his favorite and Morgan would do anything to measure up in his eyes."

"Including letting the old fart diddle her."

"That's right. She secretly hated her sister and screwed her two boyfriends to get back at her." The traffic started to move again. "Want to waste some time next week? Go visit Lenny. Maybe he'll open up now that the case is closed and Morgan is collateral damage. How much do you want to bet that Morgan saw him professionally way before she ever started screwing him? You know, patient confidentiality and all. I'll bet she opened up to him. 'My father's been sexually molesting me since I turned fourteen. He makes me go down on him in exchange for paternal recognition.' Next thing you know, she's on his lap, the degenerate therapist and daddy's bad little girl. It must've been one sexually depraved crazyfest."

"Don't know how you figure these things out,

John."

"I don't know how you missed the daddy-daughter thing."

"I was focused on trying to figure out if she committed murder. I wasn't taking notes on her psychological history at the time."

"That was the best time to take notes."

I saw his face stiffen. "What am I gonna do without you, Johnny Mocha? You and your nutty way of looking at the world. You're the best damn detective I've ever known."

A jumbo jet passed overhead. "We must be getting close to the airport." I saw the sign for the JFK Expressway a moment later. "Now don't go getting all goofy on me. This is the way God wants it."

"I can come out and visit for a couple of days, John. I've got PTO up the ass."

I felt my throat tightening. "Not a chance, you sentimental clown. Think I want you to see me withered up like an old prune? I'm particular about who I let see me in adult diapers."

We pulled up in front of the American Airlines terminal. "So this is it?"

"Yup."

Winslow got out of the car to open the trunk so that I could grab my bag. He handed me a wrapped box.

"What's this?"

"Open it." There was a T-shirt inside the box. It was a standard NYPD logo tee, but everyone on the squad had signed it. "We were going to get you a turtleneck but I couldn't find one on short notice."

I began to mist up. "That story my dad fed me all these years—I'm living proof, Matt, it's just an old wives tale." I checked the time. "Give me a hug, you old son of a bitch." I put my arms around him. "I'm gonna miss you, Winslow." I patted him on the belly. "Now watch the cheeseburgers, Okay? Enjoy your retirement. You, your darling wife, and your terrific kids, you all deserve it."

"I don't know how to tell you how much you mean to me, John."

I kissed him on the cheek the way my old man kisses me. "There's no need for you to say anything, my friend. *Acta non verba.*"

He looked at me strangely. "What? More Latin?"

"Pull out your smart phone and look it up."

And while he was searching for the answer I walked off and disappeared.

First class check-in was a breeze. I was a true neophyte when it came to the ways of the rich and had allowed way more time than I needed. So I spent the time watching people pass by. Cops are notorious people watchers. It's something we can't help, just part of our makeup I guess. I sized up everyone at the gate to kill time while we waited to board. I had labeled a would-be arsonist, an embezzler, and a low-level drug dealer before I stopped myself.

Whoa, Johnny Boy, that part of your life is over.

I suppose that having a suspicious nature was what kept me safe all the years I performed a very dangerous job, but it had also made me think in a very distinctive way, always closing doors instead of opening them and shutting out loved ones who deserved much more of me.

I'd been a confident cop, self-assured, and yes, even cocky, but as a father...

I stared down at the first class ticket I still held in my hand, and flashed back to all those lottery tickets strewn across Jessica Shannon's desk. An unsolved piece of the mystery, something I'd never know the answer to. Why was she scratching enough tickets to choke a horse, even though she was already rich?

It didn't matter, I realized. None of it did. Not

anymore. Only the ticket in my hand mattered. Maybe the odds on fixing things with my little girl were as long as the odds on the lottery tickets scattered across a dead woman's apartment, but somehow I didn't think so.

Only time would tell if I'd be able to squeeze a lifetime of happiness from the short while I'd have with Sophia. After all, I hadn't exactly been the best father, but I was determined to live out the rest of my time a better man.

The riddle I'd left with Winslow summed up why he was such a great husband and father. He was my best friend, a man I should've tried harder to emulate.

"*Acta non verba*," I whispered to myself, "Deeds, not words."

ACKNOWLEDGMENTS

No matter how self-reliant or how much of an OCD control freak any author might be, no novel comes to fruition without the benevolent help of others. The authors recognize this, and we'd like to thank:

Isabella Kelter, the unsung hero of this project, who quietly read on late into the night to make sure it was the best it could be.

Brian Triplett (R.I.P.) and John Emery, for reading a draft and going the extra mile when it comes to feedback.

Kristi Scalise, for seeing the big picture and telling it true.

ABOUT THE AUTHORS

Lawrence Kelter is the author of several bestselling mysteries and thrillers. Learn more about him at lawrencekelter.com and my-cousin-vinny.com.

Frank Zafiro was a police officer from 1993 to 2013. He is the author of more than thirty crime novels. In addition to writing, Frank is an avid hockey fan and a tortured guitarist. He lives in Redmond, Oregon. You can keep up with him at http://frankzafiro.com.

Made in the USA
Las Vegas, NV
17 June 2021